CW01085417

London · New York · Sydney

Craig Zerf
Plob fights back

© 2013, Author
Small Dog Publishing Limited

Who is Craig Zerf?

Craig wrote his first novel at the age of four and, by age seven, he was one of the most prolific writers in the Northern hemisphere. Unfortunately none of these tomes was published. This rejection forced him into seeking a career in the Dark Arts of business management. His unhealthy obsession with medieval bladed weapons and riveted metal clothing caused his initial fast rise in the corporate world to be curtailed when it was recommended by senior management that he seek professional help.

He told them to sod off and wrote Plob instead.

He has now published a trio of award-winning fantasy/humour books in the Plob series and also writes best-selling thriller novels as C. Marten-Zerf.

As Craig Zerf
Plob
Plob goes south
Plob srikes back

As C. Marten-Zerf
The Broken Men
Choice of Weapon

For Mom and Dad and Shirl…
Because with them – the pubs are always open.

We must be prepared to make heroic sacrifices for the cause of peace that we make ungrudgingly for the cause of war. There is no task that is more important or closer to my heart – **Albert Einstein**

PLOB fights back

The third hilarious fantasy/comedy
Prologue

Right - let's look at it this way. Infinity is a really difficult concept to fully understand. In fact it is said that the notion of infinity is beyond the human ability to comprehend. Even beyond the ability of the seriously bright humans who ambulate around in wheelchairs and have electronically synthesized voices.

One could try to explain it using concepts such as The Continuum and the Aleph-Null Number but when it comes down to it, all that we really need to know is that infinity is big. Really big. Imagine something egotistically huge…okay, now double it. Now double it again. You're still not even close to infinity.

Here's another way to look at the concept. Picture a giant Redwood tree. You know, one of those arrogantly large ones that are big enough to be able to carve a motor vehicle sized tunnel through. Got it? Now - cut the tree down…using only a moustache. Time it in seconds. It's going to take a while…not an infinite amount of seconds but I am sure that you get the picture.

Now - take whatever that number is and imagine this; that is how many alternative universes are out there. So many, in fact, that it is said that there is another one that is exactly like the one that we are currently in, except, and this is important, you are wearing a red shirt. (Unless, of course you are already actually wearing a red shirt - then you would be wearing a green one - probably.)

And Typhon the Dark knew this. For those of you who have not yet had the dubious pleasure of meeting the Big T before, we shall paint a vista. A written identikit.

Approximately seven feet tall, a face like a were-lizard caught halfway between the change from man to lizard, skin like a crocodile, talons like Wolverine and massive leathern wings of the bat-like variety.

Also - Typhon was a big name in the Evil business. And, like any other villain worth their salt, he was bent on world domination. Any world, he wasn't fussy. However, of late, he had become obsessed with one world in particular. That was the world that contained the despicable, the awful, the pain-in-the-buttocks-ful Plob. Magician's assistant to Smegly the master magician. Twice now Plob had thwarted the demon's plans.

But - the last time it had been close. Very close. And the major reason for that had been Typhon's acquisition of a platoon of Nazis complete with a King Tiger tank. Since then he had been scouring the multiverses, via his state of the art scrying screen, in an attempt to find the third Reich and once again to team up with them.

Thus far he had had no luck, however, Typhon knew, due to the massive choice (see moustache theory) that he had, there was every chance that, although he might not find the original Nazis, he would come across some nation that was very similar. Perhaps even badder.

So he and his team of goblins kept a permanent watch on, scouting, flicking between universes. Seeing much.

And when they found their new allies…well, let's put it this way - No more mister nice guy.

Chapter 1

They smelt. Not a wholly unpleasant smell but still a pretty powerful one. Sweaty horse with a base note of sulphur and a top note of cinnamon.

It was a smell that was uniquely Dragon.

People had been keeping, training and flying dragons for hundreds of years now but it was primarily a hobby for the wealthy or the extreme sports fanatic.

They were expensive, rare and difficult to train. But master Smegly had done some work for Duke Demorly who had been so pleased with the results that he had given the master magician a fully trained dragon as a bonus and Smegly, who was now more than successful enough to afford to keep one, had accepted. And then given it to Plob for his sixteenth birthday.

The young teenager was taken aback to say the least. It's not every day that one is gifted with a two ton, fire breathing, whole cow eating flying beast. He had named it Nimbus and called it Nim for short.

He wasn't one hundred percent sure if he actually loved the dragon, it was slow witted and stubborn. But he loved the flying. And he was really good at it.

It was the closest that man could get to feeling like a god. Part exultation, part concentration and part fear. On the slightly-down-side he was a little disappointed with the dragons flame. It was more sooty-coal-stove than the erupting volcano that he had expected. A sort of fiery burp with lots of black smoke. Apparently the flame was more part of the mating ritual than it was an aggressive weapon.

Another expectation that had gone unrealised was - girls. Plob had assumed, hopefully, that the dragon would have them lining up to talk to him but, sadly, it didn't help much. Firstly because the dragon smelt so weird and secondly because it tried to eat any girl that came too close. Master Smegly had said that was genetic. Something to do with dragons and princesses.

Plob finished rubbing Nim down with oil and gave him a quick scratch above his eye ridge. The dragon purred with a sound like an approaching avalanche. Plob patted it on the head, gave it a lump of coal for a treat, closed the door to the stable and left for the night. He was looking forward to a good night's sleep because tomorrow the three day Maudlin City royal festival started and it promiscd to be great fun.

Chapter 3

Herr Adolf Spitler was dead and the entire fatherland was in mourning. Vagoth soldiers and citizens lined the streets of the city of Lutetia. Brown jacketed members of the secret police wandered through the crowd, checking that mourners were showing a quantity of grief befitting the death of their glorious leader.

As a result the repines outward expressions of angst and woe were so over the top as to appear comedic. Breasts were beaten, teeth were gnashed and hair was rent. Tears aplenty were forced and noses ran freely with great gobs of snot. Blubs were blubbered and lambs were lamented and cats were caterwauled. The people were showing about as much genuine emotion as a bunch of three year olds crying for more sweets.

In other words, the Fuhrer's funeral was fast favouring farce.

On a raised platform, overlooking the spectacle, stood three men. On their heads were caps of black with silver skulls emblazoned thereon.

The first, Martin Boredman, was dressed in black and silver. The deceased Fuhrer's personal (very personal) secretary and general assistant who had brought back the good old-fashioned meaning of privy councillor. He was clean-shaven and, if one looked closely, one could see that he was wearing foundation, a little rouge and mascara. His hairline started on the middle of the top of his head but there was little bare skin showing as it was well covered by a pair of the universes bushiest eyebrows. Like large hamsters they were. Siberian hamsters. But with no feet. Or eyes. Or other hamstery bits. But the hamster shaped hair was there for all to see. Big bloody eyebrows is what I'm getting at. Huge.

Next to hamster-head stood the grossly obese form of Herman Gobling. Clad in a tunic and trousers of a delicate sky blue with more gold trimmings than a newly ensconced African dictator. The balding blond behemoth was in charge of the Vagoth dragon corps and his pink cherubic face and obscenely large sensual lips hid a mind as quick and merciless as a steel trap.

And finally, Josef Gooballs. Minister of propaganda and head of the cheese board. He wore his customary poo-brown tunic and pants with little adornment. Tiny, wire-rimmed glasses offset his tiny head and tiny body to perfection. He stood perhaps four foot four in built up shoes and walked with a profound limp due to a crippled right leg. But to bring attention to his diminutive size was to invite a late-night visit from the secret police. A visit that would, more often than not, involve the recipient of said visit being "cut down to size" – literally. The unusual quantity of prosthetic-limb-wearing, crutch wielding nonopeds and monopeds was stark proof of leadership that was both harsh but fair. Although the losers of said lower limbs might find the "fair" a bit of a grey area, having been so seriously caught short – as it were.

And then, with a flourish of trumpets and a fanning of fares did a jet-black bier led by six black horses hove into view. The crowd of mourners did Ooh and Aah and then some did say - Huh?

Gobling leant towards Boredman. 'Why is the coffin so small?' He asked, sotto voce.

Boredman shrugged. 'How the hell should I know? Gooballs organised the whole thing.'

The big man in blue turned the other way. 'Herr

Gooballs, why the teeny coffin?'

'It's a normal size,' hissed the little cripple. 'I measured it myself. Four foot five inches. More than adequate for any proper, average, normal sized human being.'

'Rubbish,' disagreed Gobling, secure in the fact that late night visits from secret police did not happen to Air Marshall's of the Vagoth flying corps. 'There's no way the Fuhrer could have fitted into that. What did you do, fold him in half?'

If looks could kill, the one that Herr Gooballs gave the Air Marshal would have been classed as a weapon of mass destruction. 'He fitted fine. He is a normal size in a normal coffin and he fitted in the normal way. Enough now. Watch, we are about to release one thousand doves. You'll like this, very dramatic, we had them all painted black and red to signify mourning.'

And sure enough, a line of twenty soldiers stepped forward and lined the street next to the passing bier. As one they flung open the boxes that they were carrying and from them came…nothing. Twenty soldiers stood in a row holding twenty boxes, each containing fifty doves that had long since died of lead poisoning from the layers of paint that had been slathered over them.

In a panic, one of the soldiers grabbed a handful of expired avians and tossed them hopefully into the air. The rest of the soldiers followed suit causing a shower of dead birds to rein down on the bier and the horses pulling it.

The lead horse took umbrage at being defiled by a deluge of dead doves and decided to decamp. Rearing up in his traces he darted forward only to get tangled with the horse next to him. The two stallions bit and kicked and fought, surging from side to side eventually causing the diminutive coffin to slide from the bier and go crashing to the street, splitting open on the cobbles.

There was a collective gasp of horror from the crowd as the body of the Fuhrer rolled out of the coffin to lie face down in the street. It became immediately apparent how the ex-leader had been custom fitted to the Gooballs sized coffin. The corpse's trousers were patently empty below the knees and the divorced appendages had been crammed into the coffin alongside the foreshortened body.

A large shaggy dog took advantage of the situation to lope over and grab one of the loose legs, running off with the ragged stump hanging from its drooling jaws.

'Stop it,' shrieked Herr Gooballs. 'The dog is eating the Fuhrer.'

Brown shirted policemen pushed though the crowd as they chased down the running canine.

From the raised platform Gooballs shouted commands, attempting to direct seven or eight policemen at the same time. 'No, go left. Left, left. My left, not your left, you buffoon. There, go straight. Behind you, in front of you, next to you. The other left.'

Policemen were running into each other, falling over, standing with puzzled looks on their face or, in one case, simply running around in a tight circle with their eyes closed.

Eventually the inept pursuers cornered the dog and one of the policemen wrested the leg away, holding it aloft for all to see.

'Where is the shoe?' Shouted Gooballs. 'Where is the Fuhrers shoe?'

The policeman shrugged.

'Find it. Someone has stolen the Fuhrer's shoe. Check every one legged person here.'

The brown shirts immediately turned on the many monopeds in the crowd and started to roughly search them, kicking their crutches away and frisking them to see if they were carrying any surplus footwear.

Eventually one policeman cried out. 'Here,' he called as he held the shoe above his head.

'That's not it, you moron.'

'How do you know, Herr Gooballs?'

'It's a woman's high heel pump.'

Another policeman held an object high. 'Herr Gooballs.'

'No. Wrong.'

'Why?'

'It's a right hand glove, you brown-shirted imbecile. We're looking for the Fuhrer's shoe.'

Another brown shirt called out. 'Here, here, here.'

Gooballs looked. 'No.'

'How can you be so sure, Herr Gooballs.'

'I can see that it's your shoe, cretin.'

'How can you tell from so far away?'

'It's still on your foot.'

The policeman had the decency to look embarrassed.

'Forget the bloody shoe,' urged Gobling. 'Let's just get the Fuhrer back in the little coffin and put him in the ground.'

'Yes, please. This is very upsetting,' agreed Boredman who was close to tears.

Gooballs screeched more instructions and the brown shirts bundled Spitlers's body back into the broken coffin, pushing his detached limbs down the sides.

The horses were calmed down and the procession continued. Mourners were encouraged to go back to mourning, as opposed to sniggering, and a short while of solemnity ensued.

And then the dragon corps did a fly past. A 'V' shaped formation of twenty dragons powering through the air, some two hundred foot above the crowds, belching flaming balls of fire in front of them. They turned as one and powered back, once again spitting flaming balls of burning plasma into the atmosphere. Once again there was much Oohing and Aahing and then the lead dragon decided to evacuate his bowels in quite spectacular fashion over the concentrated throng of the bereaved. The Oohs changed quickly to Eeks and there was a mad Hillsborough-like dash for cover.

Boredman burst into tears and dabbed at his eyes with a black lace handkerchief, Gobling went puce with embarrassment and Herr Gooballs limped from the podium in disgust.

The goblin scuttled down the main tunnel. His claws clicked on the cold clammy cavern floor as he coursed as quickly as he could to carry his communiqué to his master.

His master, Typhon the Dark. Capital T and capital D. The big man in the evil business.

'Master,' he said as he entered Typhon's private domain. 'I have found them.'

Typhon unfurled from the recliner that he was sprawled on. 'Are you sure?'

The goblin wrung his hands together. 'Not completely, your bigness. But very similar at least.'

'Do they have big bang things? Tanks, guns, whatever and such?'

The goblin shook his head. 'I don't think so, you monstrosityness.'

'Then you waste my time. Go away and punish

yourself. Thirty lashes should do. Then rub salt in the wounds and deny yourself tea for a few days.'

The goblin blanched at the thought of going tea-less for so long. 'But, sir. They have dragons.'

'Dragons'

Typhon raised an eyebrow. 'What, those big fat flying lizards that blow smoke? So what?'

'No, my master. These ones were different. Men flew them with great precision and they fired huge balls of flame. Scary they were. And impressive. The people watching did go Ooh. And Aah.'

'Show me.'

So he took him to the scrying screen and did so. And the big T was mightily impressed. Massed troops. Fire spitting dragons. Men with death's head insignia on their uniforms. Brown shirted men beating up cripples. All the ingredients that he was looking for.

He patted the goblin on the head. 'Well spotted. Now, prepare my best armour and a personal bodyguard detachment of ten Ogres in full battle gear, axes and morningstars. It is time to pay a visit on these peoples and make them an offer that they can't refuse.'

Herr Gooballs limped up the stairs to his private apartment. He had taken leave of the fat man and the fey man. A little alone time was what he needed, a drink and a long hot bath. With bubbles. And toys.

You see, Gooballs was perturbed, to say the least. The untimely death of the Fuhrer had left an unfillable vacuum in the Vagoth political structure. The Vagoths needed a strong leader. Someone who could make decisions. Gooballs was enough of a realist to know his own shortcomings and leading was one of them. He was a brilliant propagandist and strategist but he would never hold the hearts and minds of the people.

Boredman was out of the question, far too emotional and prone to random outbursts of hysterics. As for the flying fat man - he was bright enough, but was so narcissistic as to border on the very edge of insanity. In fact his entire apartment had all of the walls covered in mirrors so as to reflect and re-reflect an infinity of images of himself back and forth, so that he could simply stand and stare in wonder at them. Gooballs was not sure what the fat man saw but he suspected that his mind's eye had trimmed down the reality somewhat and added a few muscles and thickened the straggly blond hair somewhat.

The little cripple snorted in disgust. The self-delusion of some people was beneath contempt. He unlocked the door to his apartment and went in.

At first glance there seemed to be nothing unusual about Herr Gooballs's living quarters. They were sumptuous and displayed an abundance of fine arts and priceless tapestries, but apart from that it was a patently normal apartment. The chairs, tables and counters - all decidedly normal.

And, after pausing to think a while…that very normality is what gives the game away. Typically, Herr Gooballs would enter a room and something odd would become immediately apparent vis-à-vis the relative scale of the room. *Id est,* either the room and contents appeared larger than life or it was obvious that the man who had just entered was of a diminutive nature.

As a result of this feeling of constant vertical belittlement Herr Gooballs had had his personal rooms hand made in a 1:2 scale which made his relative height grow from four foot two inches to eight foot four. Even his crockery and cutlery had been scaled down. And his bath products. To further enhance his personal feeling of apparent hugeness, Herr Gooballs would often walk about his apartment in slow motion and make assorted swishing and crumping and stomping noises to accompany his giant footsteps.

'Fee…Guramph.   Fi…Gudoof.   Foe…Fagluph. Fum…Badoink.'

The little man loved his private rooms.

He drew himself a bath, poured in a copious amount of bubble mixture, shed his clothes and lowered himself in. The mass of bubbles covered him completely as he lay back, relaxing in the hot water and soapy froth. After a while he cleared his throat and started to sing. For some unbeknown reason Herr Gooballs favoured a squeaky, Bee Gees, Monty Pythonesque 'I'm a lady' type falsetto.

'All these hypocrites we throw them out,
Goblins leave our Vagoth house,
If the native soil is clean and pure,
Happy and united we endure.'

The little minister punctuated each line with a bout of aquatically enhanced flatulence that reverberated off the cast iron tub like a sounding board.

And for a while Herr Gooballs was truly happy as he wallowed in his bath with his miniature soaps and tiny bottles of shampoo, singing Vagoth songs whilst his turds whistled for right of way.

His reverie was interrupted by a frantic banging on his front door. 'Herr Gooballs.'

'Who is it?'

'It's me. Sergeant Shultzenmoltenhausen.'

'Go away.'

'I have a message for you, Herr minister, it is urgent.'

'Well slide it under the door.'

Gooballs arose from the bubble bath and donned a sumptuous white towelling robe and a pair of built-up slippers. Then he went to the door and opened it.

Lying on the floor in front of the door, blood streaming from a gash in his head was sergeant Shultzenmoltenhausen.

'What the hell are you doing, sergeant?'

'Trying to push the message under the door, Herr minister.'

'So what is so difficult about that?'

'Please, sir. The message is in my head.'

'Tell me quickly and then get a bucket and a mop and clean this blood up, you imbecilic clodpate.'

'Herr Gobling needs you at the Führerhauptquartiere. We have a visitor.'

'Who is it?'

'I have no idea, Herr minister. May I go now, sir? I think that some of my brain has come out.'

Gooballs waved the hapless sergeant away and went back into his rooms to don his uniform.

A short while later he ushered himself into the main boardroom at the FHQ. And what he saw there filled him with surprise. And shock. And more than a little bit of fear.

Chapter 4

August.
1940.
England.
The British airmen called it 'first light'. That barely discernable lightening of the sky. Not yet dawn but no longer night. They sat in the dispersal hut, huddled over fast cooling mugs of sweet tea. Some smoked. None talked. They waited.

First light. The rim of the sun edged slowly over the horizon. Not smoothly but in small incremental movements. As if it were embarrassed. Uncomfortable that it brought with it another day. Another eighteen hours of light. And with it, another eighteen hours of combat. And death.

First light. Sheepskin lined leather flying jackets were shrugged on in preparation. Pipes knocked out. Time stretched thin, like piano wire. And then the bell rang; a call to arms. Instructions shouted out. "Bandits coming in over the cliffs. Forty heavies and twenty fighters. Angels eighteen". Mugs knocked over, spilt tea shining on the tabletops. Men up and running. Boot shod feet pounded the damp turf. Ground crew standing by ready to help the flyers up and strap them in.

First light. The smell of petrol in the air. The blaring of the twenty-seven litre Rolls Royce Merlin engines as the chocks were pulled away and throttles were thrown open. Seeking flight.

And then the thundering engines, powering five thousand pounds of airplane into the air.

Eight .303 machine guns, 1030 BHP, one proud young airman.

The destructive power of Britain's greatest

fighter – the Spitfire.

The flight of four Spitfires had taken off from Biggin Hill in Kent and consisted of flight lieutenant Samuel 'Smudger' Smith, flying officer Jonathan 'Jonno' Johnson, flying officer Reginald 'Belter' Bridgestone and the new Polish addition, pilot officer Rufin Kowolski.

'Righty-ho, gentlemen,' said Smudger over the radio. 'The Huns are coming in at angels eighteen so let's try to get our birds up to twenty thousand feet and get some sort of height advantage.'

'Roger, Smudge,' confirmed Jonno.

'Wilco, skipper,' replied Belter.

'Hupsydaisy, one more for the shoebox,' said Rufin.

Smudger ignored the Polish pilot's seeming transgression of radio protocol. This was because Smudger, and everyone else in the flight, was well aware that the Pole was in the process of learning English.

The odd thing about Rufin was that he had an eidetic, or photographic memory as well as an incredible ability to mimic sounds and syntax. Because of this he had managed, in an unbelievably short time, to learn pretty much every word in the English lexicon, but he had yet to learn what order to put them in. As a result, he tended to communicate in meaningless strings of perfectly pronounced English words and phrases.

The Spits powered on up towards their twenty four thousand foot ceiling, using up petrol at a prodigious rate.

After twenty minutes Smudger saw them. 'Bandits eight o'clock, angles eighteen,' he called.

'I see them, skip.'

'I'm on them, Smudger.'

'Away with the melons, aunty.'

And the flight swooped down on the enemy at odds of over twelve-to-one against.

Chapter 5

Plob wandered through the grounds of the fair eating a toffee apple on a stick. It was day one of the three-day festival that had been declared to celebrate the birth of king Bravad R Us' first child to queen Dreenee. A son that had been named Bravad Aswel.

A group of travelling carnivals had set up on the outskirts of the city along with the usual rides and sideshows and Plob had spent the morning checking things out.

Master Smegly had given Plob the whole three days off, bar helping him during the magician's contest on the second day. Also, Plob had to conclude the third day with a dragon fly-past featuring the local flying club of five dragons and the young magician was going to the dragon pens to make sure that Nim was comfortable and had enough peat in his feedbag. He decided to take a short cut behind the carnie's caravans so that he could get to the pens quicker.

He turned the corner to see a group of singlet clad, tattooed, wiry muscled carny tent pitchers and handlers. There were six of them clustered around a skinny teenage boy who looked vaguely as if he were composed entirely of knees and elbows. His tunic and trews were too short, leaving six inches of pale, malnourished ankle and wrist extending from the material like bleached twigs wrapped in cloth. The carnies were laughing and pushing him from person to person. The gangling boy staggered and spun from hand to hand. Eventually he fell to the floor and lay there, staring up at his intimidators with a puzzled expression.

One of the carnies kicked him. Not hard. Not even with aggression. Merely with casual contempt for someone who was not as physically able as he was. This was greeted with more ribald laughter.

Plob had never been bullied. From an early age he had been apprenticed to mater Smegly and had spent many a laborious hour at the furnace, hammering raw magic into spells. As a result he was built like a blacksmith and had been since his fourteenth birthday. This, added to the fact that he was a very accomplished magician who had already been involved in literal life and death battles numerous times, made him an adversary that it was best to avoid. However - these people were not locals so were unaware of these facts.

He strode forward, shouldered his way past the carnies and lifted the boy to his feet. Now he was closer he could see that the boy was not as young as he had at first thought. Probably fifteen, but seriously undernourished.

Someone tapped Plob on the shoulder. 'Hey, you. Bugger off.'

The teenage magician turned to look at the speaker. A face like a police brutality poster. Broken teeth, crooked nose, ridge of scar tissue across the eyebrows and breath that would curl a corpse's toes at a hundred yards. His arms looked like they had been put together with flesh coloured cables and skin. He stood perhaps three inches over Plob's six feet.

'Give us your toffee apple and piss off, pretty boy, before I get angry.' This was greeted with much laughter and wolf whistles from the rest of the group.

Plob knew the score. There would be a trading of insults, a bit of pushing and shoving and then the whole bunch would attack him. But he was a well brought up boy and thought that he should at least give them a chance to apologise.

He held up his hand. 'I am leaving with my

24

friend. You will apologise, you will stand aside and you will let us leave. These are the last words that I will say to you.'

'Oh, really? What you going to do, kiss me to death?' There was more laughter but this time it was a little subdued. Almost nervous. There was something about this teenager that simply didn't add up.

Plob had already given fair warning so felt entirely justified in reacting the way that he did. He cocked his fist and drove a straight right into bad-breath's face, hitting him so hard that he cartwheeled backwards into the side of a caravan with a sound like a watermelon smashing open on a pavement. Then he muttered a quick air-fire incantation, released it and pulled the boy to safety as a miniature bolt of lightning crackled from carny to carny, frazzling hair, burning off eyebrows and knocking them, twitching and drooling, to the ground.

Plob continued to the pens with the boy lolloping next to him.

'What's your name, boy?'

'Boy.'

'Yes, you. Your name?'

'Boy.'

'So, is that what everyone calls you?'

'Naw.'

'What do they call you then?'

'Youweeshitebuggeroff.'

'Okay…Boy it is then.'

'Sir, where we settin' foot ta?'

Plob had to concentrate a little to get his brain around the accent. 'To see my dragon.'

'Ah lik' dragons.'

Plob handed Boy the rest of his toffee apple. Boy ate it in two bites. Then he ate the stick.

'Hungry?' Asked Plob.

Boy nodded.

'When did you last eat?'

Boy shrugged. 'A while back. Day afore yesterday, I think.'

'When we're finished here I'll find you something to eat.'

Boy nodded.

'Well,' said Plob. 'We're here.' Plob lead Boy into the set of six pens. Five were occupied and Nim was in the first pen on the left. 'Now be careful. Nim gets very jealous and tends to bite.'

Boy walked straight up to the dragon and scratched it under its massive chin. 'Ach, ye braw wee thing. How urr ye?'

Nim purred like an avalanche and licked Boy's face with his two-foot long, sticky black tongue. Plob was amazed. Never before had he seen Nim react so favourably to a stranger. In fact, it was unusual for any dragon to so friendly first off.

'He likes you.'

'Aye, al dragons like me. Ah grew up wi' thaim.'

'So, where are you from, Boy?'

'Ah wis born in th' hills o' Bracolgoght in th' Northern realms.'

Plob started to fill Nim's feedbag with fresh peat. 'I wondered about the accent. But I thought that you guys all wore skirts.'

'They're nae skirts, they're kilts.'

'Well why aren't you wearing one?'

'Cripes, ah git beat up enough as it's. Whit dae ye think mah life wid be lik' if ah wore a dress?'

'Kilt.'

'Och, whatever.'

'So, Boy, can you fly?'

'Nae. Could never afford to.'

'Do you know how it works?'

Boy shrugged.

'Here,' said Plob. 'Take a look. You steer via this set of rope and pulleys that we attach to the saddle. Then we run the rope along these sets of steel rings that are pierced through the leading edge of the dragon's wings. Then we connect that same rope to the stirrups. So if you push down on the stirrup it pulls the corresponding wing in, causing the dragon to turn in that direction. You relax your foot and flight continues straight and level. Push both stirrups down and the dragon dives. Thump your heels into its flanks and it climbs. Squeeze your knees it goes faster. Simple.'

In reality Plob knew that flying was actually anything but simple. In fact it was more akin to trying to scratch your nose with your elbow while carrying a rabid dog from a burning building. Complicated and dangerous.

'Well, I'm finished here,' continued the young magician. 'Let's go take a look at the fair and see if we can get you something more substantial than a toffee apple.'

'Thank ye muchly, sir.'

Plob led Boy away and they went in search for comestibles.

Chapter 6

Typhon was amazed. Astonished. And astounded. He was also glad, gleeful and gratified. No - not strong enough…he was more than glad, he was, in fact, ecstatic, elated…euphoric even. And the reason for this was; he was winning. After a series of quite serious setbacks in his recent past things were now going, almost uncontrollably, his way. And…it…was…GOOD!

Afore him was arrayed the mighty army of the Vagoths. Pikemen and swordsmen and bowmen and engines of war. And to his left stood Herr Gobling and Herr Boredman. To his right, the little Gooballs. It had been the quickest transfer of power that Typhon had ever heard of.

He had entered their realm with ten ogre bodyguards with the intention of organising a bit of power sharing in mind. A little, I scratch your back, you tear off Plob's back and burn his cities to the ground, type of thing. But it was almost as if the Vagoths needed to be led. They had lived for so long under the yoke of their former Fuhrer, who was, as far as the big T could tell, a complete and utter nutcase, that they were incapable of leading themselves.

Pretty much everything that Typhon had suggested was fast agreed on (as long as it involved war, destruction, mayhem and dressing up in black uniforms with loads of death's head badges and lightning bolts).

Now he stood before the horde as they all threw their arms straight above their heads and honoured him with the traditional salute. 'Hey-oop, Herr

Typhon. Hey-oop!'

But the thing that excited him the most. The reason that he shivered with multiple frissons of pleasure as he stood in front of the mighty multitude of militants, was the dragons. A score's score and a bit more they numbered. (Work it out…a score is twenty. Okay? Twenty multiplied by another score makes four hundred. Add a bit more and you get; a lavatory full of dragons, like…umm…lots).

Not the smoky, little noxious burp-of-flame producers that were prevalent on Typhon's world were these beasts. Oh no. These dragons spat fire that burned as hot as the sun and travelled as fast as a bolt of lightning. The pilots that sat atop them were impressive, clad in sadomasochistic costumes of black leather and fur. They ruled the skies as knights of the air. And these smelting steeds and their searing sea of flames would bring on the decisive demise of Plob and his fellow denizens. So, ha. Take that. And that and that.

Boy ate like a person possessed.

A person possessed by a sumo wrestler after a day of fasting. Plob had purchased a tub of stew from one of the food stalls. The dish was listed as the "Mystery Meat Gut-Buster…feed the family for less than a Dollar." They had sat down at one of the rough wooden tables provided and Boy had set to.

Plob watched with amazement. Boy ate with a strange sort of deftness. He used the two handed method, whilst one hand was inserting food into mouth the other was scooping more up in readiness. Shoulders swayed slightly from side to side and jaws masticated rhythmically. The Gut-Buster went down in an incredibly short time.

'Full?'

'Ta, a'm stowed oot.'

'Let's go check out the sights.'

Plob and Boy wandered aimlessly around the various stalls and sideshows at the fair. Boy ate another three toffee apples and a sausage in a bun. Then he ate something grapefruit sized and pink and sweet that had been rolled in sugar and syrup and honey and desiccated coconut and more sugar, and then left lurking under a glass dome waiting for someone like Boy. It stained his teeth, his hands, his tunic and, somehow the soles of his socks a virulent pink.

The two of them decided to have another look at the hairiest woman in the world again, even though it was patently a badly shaved bear, because it wasn't something that you got to see every day.

Plob heard him before he saw him. Shouting across the crowd with a voice like rolling thunder. 'Who dat buckaballer dat I sees dere? Is dat my good friend Plob?' And then he hove into view. Seven foot tall, over three hundred pounds of muscle, massive teeth protruding from an overshot jaw, shaggy brown fur and a grin that stretched so wide it looked like he was about to swallow his own ears.

'Biggest.'

Boy took an inadvertent step back. 'Wassat?'

'That's Biggest. He's a Trogre, a cross between a troll and an ogre. We're old friends.'

Biggest cut through the crowd like a runaway ocean liner, picked Plob up and spun him around. 'Hey, Plob, how youse doing? I aint seended you since the donkey was young.'

'I'm good, Big, I'm good. This is a friend, Boy.'

Biggest engulfed Boy's hand in his paw. 'Right on, Boy. How doody?'

'Chuffed tae meet wi` ye, Bigman.'

''Hey, youse is from those Bracolgoght peoples. Da ones dat wear skirts. What tribe?'

'A'm fram the McGethastiched tribe. And they're called kilts.'

'So, Big. What you doing in this neck of the woods?'

'I came to see Bravad and Dreenee and do some oohing and aahing over da baby.'

'So what you been up to since we last were together?'

'Started a business wid my brothers. We do's security work. Based in da town of Widless. We does bounty huntin, debt collectin. If you pays us den we can track down da miscreants for youse and, for a little extra, we's can bash dem inna noggin till blobby bits comes out dere ears. We call da business "Biggest and Bros for Bargain Basement Bonce Bashing" - It's good work, we's doing well and we enjoys it. Specially da bashing of da bonces.'

'Have you seen Mater Smegly yet?'

'Negative.'

'Well follow me; let's give him a shout. Come on, Boy, stick with us.'

Wing Captain Count Wolfgang Peesundbakon felt his reticence drain from him like spit from a spastic. This new Fuhrer that had been foisted upon them by the triumvirate of leaders was actually turning out to be a bit of all right.

A little odd looking, what with the scaly skin, the wings, claws and lizard-face. But at least he didn't foam at the mouth like the last one. Also, he didn't seem as obsessed with killing off all of the goblins in the motherland. Most importantly, he saw that the Vagoths were a warrior race and that they had run out of enemies to conquer on their world and so had come up with an entire new world to lay waste. And he had promised them a way to get there.

The new Fuhrer had control over magiks hereto unseen by the Vagoths, and this magic allowed them to travel between their world and the next. The only downside was that the amount of people travelling at once was rather limited. Fifty or so being the said limit. He was, however, working on this.

This very morning the count had been called to see the Fuhrer together with the dragon forces top four pilots; Hulbert Hanselunddgretal, Pieter Spittleundflem, Albret Pawksosaje, and Hienz Beenz. They were told that they had the honour of being the first flight of dragons into the new world. They were to do a little reconnaissance and, if possible, take out all and any enemies that dared to cross their path.

Wolfgang was looking forward to chance to earn himself some more medals. Already he was the holder of the Iron Cross with Oak leaves, tinsel and silver baubles. He was keen to add the coveted small blue fuzzy thing to it and become the highest decorated flyer in the Vagoth's military history.

Typhon finished his speech. And a good one it was too. Full of Motherlands and Lebensraums and Death-Before-Dishonours. The crowd went wild with the two-handed salutes and the Hey-oops echoed around the plaza.

The Vagoth flags rippled in the wind, the red mailed fist on black striking pride into his warrior's heart. The Bumsenfaust logo was known and either feared or loved by all. Above their heads, in a show of aerial might, flew a wing of the Fokker-class fighter dragons together with a wing of the huge slow Belend-class two headed bomber dragons. The fighters whirled around the massive bombers like wasps around vultures.

Count Wolfgang Peesundbakon gave one last salute and then headed towards his quarters. It was almost time and he needed to change out of his dress uniform and into his combat gear in readiness for the flight.

Chapter 7

The forty-two Heinkle 111 bombers flew in steady at two hundred and fifty miles per hour. They had flown over the White Cliffs of Dover approximately seven minutes after first light. Some ten thousand feet above them flew a pack of over seventy Messerschmitt 109's the ubiquitous German fighter planes.

Smudger had taken his boys up to their ceiling of thirty thousand feet. Twelve spitfires. Belter saw them first and called out over the R/T. 'Bandits at eight o'clock, skipper. Messerschmitt 109's.'

'How many, Belter?'

'Umm…all of them, I think, skipper.'

'Jolly good. Enough for all of us then. Well, chaps, you know our job. Go for the heavies and watch out for the snappers coming in from above. Tally Ho, break, break, break.'

Instantly the sky broke into whirling confusion, headphones filled with shouts of command, warning, exultation…stark terror.

'Flamer, watch it he's going down.'

'Look out Jonno…Jesus, that was close.'

'He's on you tail, Smudger…wait…I'm coming in…hold. He's down. He's gone. Another one, turn, turn, turn.'

'More bombers, two o'clock. Tally ho.'

'I'm burning…help…'

'Potato and sputum. Mixed bag of nuts for the janitor,' added Rufin, his eight machine guns blazing away.

And then suddenly, in that miracle of aerial

combat, the sky was empty. A few trails of black smoke marked the downed aircraft. In the distance a parachute blossomed briefly, taking its pilot safely to ground.

'To me, gentlemen. Formation please. Let's get back to base and re-arm,' called Smudger.

The remaining Spitfires gathered into tight formation. Smudger took a quick count. Ten. They had lost two.

'Sound out, fellows. Who's gone?'

'That new chap with the blond hair,' said Jonno.

'And the short one. Big ears,' said Belter.

Smudger knew them but couldn't remember their names. New boys both. A few hours of training and bags of enthusiasm. The new ones had an average life expectancy of one week. Seven days spent either sleeping, getting drunk or flying. And, of course - dying.

Still, Smudger guessed that they had taken out at least twenty-two bombers and a dozen or so fighters so, on paper, it had been a good sortie. Of course Blondie and Big ears would disagree but that's life (or death) isn't it.

It had been two days since they had lost Blondie and Big ears and Smudger's boys had flown another four sorties. The last one had been bomber support, which, as always, was pretty hairy.

Smudger lay in bed awake. He had awoken early. Before his usual four thirty wake up call from his batman, Corporal Bedford. The timepiece on his bedside table stood at four o'clock and Smudger's head thumped in time with the ticking of its mechanisms. Slowly memories of yesterday swam to the fore. They had successfully completed their bombing mission on Hanover, leaving the railhead in smoking ruin and destroying the crossroads.

On the way back they had run into a terrible storm. But that came with its own advantages. No enemy fighters dared to take off in such foul weather. They lost another two heavies on the way back. One spiralling out of the sky over France and the other plunging into the cold grey sea, taking its crew with it to a lonely grave.

They had split from the heavies after flying over the chalk cliffs of Dover. The heavies flew on to their base at Horsham and the fighter boys touched down at the Biggin Hill. As soon as Smudger had climbed down from his Spitfire the ground crew had started refuelling and arming.

Smudger and the surviving members of B flight had been debriefed and then taken a quick shower before catching a lift to the local pub called 'The Old Jail' on one of the base's trucks.

Then they had drunk. As they did every night. And because a young man in his late teens or early twenties, at the peak of physical fitness, needs to drink an awful lot in order to forget - they drank an awful lot.

Rumour was that they would be getting a raft of new boys and kites in to strengthen the squadron over the next few days. The gods knew that they needed them. Smudger knew that none of his lads would ever admit it, but there was something very disheartening about always flying into combat against an enemy that outnumbered you at least eight or ten to one. Still, thinking about such things would only weaken one's morale and that simply wouldn't do.

He heard corporal Bedford as he stopped outside his door to balance his tea tray whilst he pushed the door open. The batman walked in, laid the tray down next to Smudger's cot and then drew the curtains back. It was still dark outside.

'I'm sorry to say that the birds are walking outside, sir,' he informed the squad leader as he sugared his tea. 'Fog's as thick as a pea soup. There'll be no going up in this I'm sad to inform.'

Smudger hid his rush of relief behind a mask of disappointment. 'Damn it all, Bedford. That simply won't do. There's cabbage heads out there for the taking and we'll be sitting on our thumbs because of a little fog. Damned shame.'

Bedford nodded in agreement. 'I told the lads. Mr Smith will be that upset, I told them. He needs his daily crack at the Vagoths like we all need food and water.' The small man puffed his chest out proudly. 'Yes, I told them, I did.'

'Vagoths, Bedford?'

The batman looked puzzled. 'I'm sorry, mister Smith, sir. I meant the Jerry. Slip of the tongue, don't even know what a Vagoth is.'

Smudger's stomach grumbled in distress as he ingested his hot tea and it took all of his strength to keep it down. But, after a few more sips he started to feel better. What he needed was a good breakfast. And then maybe he would be genuinely happy when the fog lifted. Perhaps.

Then he grinned to himself. Vagoths, whatever next?

Chapter 8

Boy helped Plob tighten the saddle cinch up, kneeing
Nim in the stomach and then pulling tight. The four
other dragon riders were lined up next to him, also
saddling up their mounts.

Master Smegly had put together a fancy
contraption that consisted of a powder and a liquid
that he had decanted into two separate containers.
These containers were then tied together and, via a
rope and a couple of pulleys, the contents would be
mixed when the rope was pulled. This resulted in a
stream of red smoke that poured out of the containers
for almost a minute. The master had strapped one of
these devices to each dragon's leg and the plan was to
pull the ropes during the flypast and then do a few
simple aerobatics and give the crowd a bit of a
spectacle.

Plob was head flyer and the others were to take
their lead from him. He mounted Nim and gave the
them all a thumbs up which was repeated by all. The
dragons lumbered forward, in formation, and then
took off, changing instantly from clumsy bumbling
beasts into graceful ships of the air.

Plob started by taking the wing up high, pulling
the ropes so that the smoke streamed out behind them
as they climbed into the clear blue skies. Then, at the
top of the climb he instituted a gentle right hand turn
and spiralled slowly down towards the ground.
Behind the five dragons the sky filled with spirals of
red smoke. The crowd cheered and clapped.

Plob took the team low over everybody's head,

low enough for them to feel the downdraft from the massive beating wings. Then another climb, spiralling up in tight turns and painting the sky with more red spirals. Again, clapping and cheering.

And then there was the sound of rolling thunder and the air seemed to shimmer with heat. The five Vagoth dragons appeared in the skies high above Plob and his team of amateur flyers. They hovered for a moment and then dove straight for the festival flyers.

Plob saw the diving dragons with his peripheral vision. Mere flickers of green and black coming out of the sun and, as he turned to look, a ball of burning plasma seared past him and struck the dragon next to him.

The dragon screeched in agony as the fire punched through its outstretched wing leaving a smoking hole. Immediately the rider lost control and the pair of them dropped out of the sky as the dragon spun to the ground.

Plob's brain shut down. The enormity of what was happening proved to be too much. Who were these people? Why were they attacking him? How was it possible for their dragons to spit fire like that? Everyone knew that dragons were only capable of emitting small, sooty flames that were barely able to toast bread let alone burn people to death.

Two more balls of fire sizzled past Plob and struck another two dragons from the sky.

And the young magician's mind came back online. He squeezed tight with both knees and thumped his heels in. Nim bunched up as he increased his speed and pulled up, flying almost vertically. Plob kept him going as hard as he could, head swivelling around as he tried to get a fix on the enemy dragons. He was surprised to see that all of his festival dragons were down. Mere smoking piles of burnt flesh on the ground.

Two of the enemy dragons were close on his tail as he continued climbing. The other three dragons were cruising over the fairground, spitting balls of fire into the crowd and wreaking untold damage to both property and life.

Plob waited until the dragons were close enough to fire at him and then he stood up in his saddle, pulling both of Nim's wings in. They went from a climb into a vertical dive. Plob kept standing until the last possible moment when he relaxed his right stirrup, unfolding Nim's wing and pulling them into a screaming right hand turn some ten feet above ground level. Nim yelped in pain as the change of direction pulled at his tendons. Plob urged him on, heading for the nearby forest. Two balls of fire streaked past and exploded into the ground in front of him. He jinked left and right in a frantic attempt to throw his attackers off but they were good flyers. Much better than him.

The forest loomed ahead. Massive Bluewood trees that stood one hundred foot tall. Plob drove Nim onwards, whipping through the trees at top speed as fireballs whistled past him, burning all in their paths. But he could feel Nim was tiring. No beast could take this speed for any protracted time period.

And then they were gone. No dragons. No balls of fire. Only hundreds of smoking fires. Plob brought Nim up to a few hundred feet and guided him slowly back to the fairground. From the air the extent of damage was immediately apparent. Burning buildings and caravans. Four dead dragons. And human bodies. Scattered as if by a giant's tantrum, twisted and broken. And burning.

All around them people rushed to help with

buckets of water and wet blankets. Even from the height he was, Plob could plainly hear the sobs and screams of agony.

He guided Nim to the landing field and put down, climbing off as he hit the ground, running to help.

Count Wolfgang Peesundbakon touched down on the landing strip and brought his dragon to a halt in two steps, a perfect landing. The other four veterans landed next to him with just as much efficiency of movement.

The ground crews swarmed around the dragons, helping the flyers down, stripping the equipment off the dragons, rubbing oil into their scales and checking for any damage. The five flyers walked to the debriefing room together. They did not look happy.

'That was ridiculous,' said the count. 'They didn't even fight back. And they were rubbish flyers. Worse than amateurs.'

'One was pretty good,' said Heinz.

There was general agreement.

'Yes,' said Hulbert. 'That crash dive was quite brilliant. I doubt that I could have done better myself.'

'But why didn't they fire back?' Asked Count Peesundbakon.

'They were too scared.'

'No. That's not it. Did you notice that they didn't even have tongue depressors fitted to their dragons? It's as if they didn't even know how to make them fire.'

The count was more than disappointed. There was no way that he was going to earn the small blue fuzzy thing to add to his iron cross if all that he did was kill amateurs and strafe women and children.

This was not looking to be as much fun as he thought it would. What he really wished for was a proper war. A war that involved strife and hardship and lots of public recognition and medals.

And, because when all things were carefully considered, count Wolfgang Peesundbakon was actually a bit of a dick, fate decided to grant him his wish.

Spice patted the earth down with the back of her shovel and then stood back. It was a good job. The wooden marker at the top stood straight and the two pieces of willow that had been tied to it were the perfect length, showing that the two people in the grave had been married and died together in their twilight years.

Spice had never known her real parents but Gungun and Papa had taken care of her since she could remember and, as such, she considered them to be her parents. They had both died of the fever within hours of each other and the teenage girl had buried them the next day.

She walked back to the small log cabin that she had called home for her whole life and went inside. She stripped and, using a cloth and a bowl of water, washed the sweat and mud from her body. She was tall for a girl, perhaps five foot eleven, and her muscles stood out, taut through her pale skin.

Her breasts were large and well formed and they set off her large dark green eyes to perfection. They also set off her feet, her hands and the small mole on her cheek to perfection. What could one say - they were perfection enhancing breasts.

She splashed water through her short hair causing it to stand up in raggedly chopped bunches, reached for a towel, dried herself and donned her leather flying outfit.

Her dragon stood outside the front door already saddled up. She stroked its eye-ridges and it crooned back at her.

'So, Tempest, we're all alone.'

The dragon butted her with its wagon-sized head and whickered. Spice patted the dragon again and then climbed aboard. She kicked her heels and Tempest flapped its wings and rose up above the log cabin. The two hovered there for a while and then Spice pulled back on Tempest's firing reins and the dragon spat a ball of fire at the cottage. It struck with the force of a lightning bolt and immediately reduced the wooden abode to cinders.

'Come on, Tempest. Let's go and start our new lives.'

And they climbed high into the sky and headed towards the capital city of Maudlin, hoping for good things and new beginnings.

Chapter 9

King Bravad had called a council of war and his major, his generals and other various notables sat with him in his chambers. The unexpected dragon raid had cost the lives of twenty-three people including ten children.

He had declared a day of mourning. But the people did not want to mourn. They wanted revenge. And answers.

'Master Smegly. Do have any idea why this happened?' Asked the king.

The magician shook his head. 'Bravad, not only do I have no idea why they did this; I also have no idea who did it. I have never seen the like of those dragons that they rode. I have no idea how they got them to shoot fire like that. Their flying skills were beyond those that I have seen before and, most disturbingly, I conjured a number of seeking spells and all that I got was that they are from very, very, very far away.' The master magician slumped down in his seat. 'I wish that I could be of more help.'

The king turned to Plob. 'My friend. Anything to add, after all, you were closest to them.'

Plob shrugged. 'I was too busy trying not to be dead to notice much. I did get the feeling that the amount of fire that they produce is limited in some way. They had me cold near the end but didn't fire. I can only assume that their dragons ran out of burn…fire…whatever.'

'Alright,' continued the king. 'I am going to

declare a state of emergency. I will call up all of the standing army and civilian militia. I want every longbow, crossbow, catapult and ballista that we have on the tops of Maudlin's city walls and all of the high buildings. I also want water troughs and barrels of water distributed to key points in the city and firemen rosters set up amongst the locals. Master Smegly, can you put together any spells that could help?'

Smegly harrumphed. 'The usual thunderbolts etcetera won't do much good. You see, when it comes down to it, an attack spell is still merely a hand-launched missile, albeit very powerful. Also, it is a well-known fact that dragons themselves are very resistant to magiks. Part of the reason that such a huge beast can fly so fast is that it generates its own small magical field that helps to keep it airborne. This tends to negate most spells. I think that I can put together a net of spells that might give us some sort of prior warning as to when they arrive. Assuming that they do come again.'

'Oh, they'll come again,' said the king. 'They will definitely come again.'

'I'll help the master with the spells,' said Plob.

'No,' said Bravad. 'I have something else for you. I need you to find out how they did what they did. How they managed to produce such hot flames from their dragons. Once you have done that then we will talk again. Right, everyone, to your tasks.'

The meeting adjourned and all filed out of the royal chambers.

'Plob,' called the king. 'Don't sleep and eat only when necessary. The kingdom is relying on you, my boy.'

Wow, thought Plob to himself as he left the room. No pressure.

It was nighttime and the young magician sat in the middle of the landing field, on a three-legged stool, and stared at Nim. He had absolutely no idea where to start. He had only seen his dragon flame before on two separate occasions. And both times had been sooty little flames that wouldn't even singe ones hair let alone destroy entire buildings.

The dragon sensed its owner's mood and bumped him with his head. Plob scratched him and he made a series of small plopping noises and then started to purr.

Suddenly an idea came to Plob. He stood up and tore one of the legs off the stool. Then he mumbled a quick incantation, gestured, and the end of the wooden leg burst into flame.

He held the flame in front of Nim. 'Here, Nim. See this?' Can you do this?' Plob waved the leg around making circles of flame in the air. Then he pushed it in Nim's face. 'Come on, Nim. Do something.'

The dragon looked at him with huge soulful eyes and then it opened its mouth and drew a huge breath.

'Yes,' encouraged Plob. 'Do it.'

Nim stood up, arched his back and with one mighty gust…blew out the fire. Then he sat back down, closed his eyes and promptly went to sleep.

Plob dropped the charred piece of wood and stood still. Shoulders down in a perfect pose of dejection.

'Bugger.'

'Wa ye doin?'

Plob turned to see Boy. He had a paper bag full of what seemed to be fried chicken, he also had a piece in his hand and was eating it like a corn on the cob, rolling and biting and chewing at the same time. Once again showing his efficiency in oral consumption.

'Nothing,' said Plob. 'Making a fool of myself.'

'Ah weel, if you need ta make a fool of yournself then you're definitely the best one ta do it. Da ya want some fried chikkie. It's reet good. I got it from Biggest.'

Plob took a leg. It was good, moist with a crisp batter.

'So, what's wit the burnt stool?'

'I was trying to get Nim to produce a hotter flame.'

'Oh, is tha' all? Tha's easy, you jist feed yon dragon with Natrium crystals. They fire up a treat mon, a reet treat,'

'What?'

'Natrium.'

'I don't know what that is.'

'Och, Natrium's a crystal. Ye find it in caves in big blocks. Looks lik' ice. You dig it oop and smash it and feed it to yon dragons. They love it; it's like sweeties to them. Makes their flames awful hot. Like the sun.'

'Boy, why didn't you tell me this before?'

Boy shrugged. 'Ye didna ask.'

'So, let me get this straight. I feed these crystals to the dragon and then I can fight back against those flyers and their dragons?'

'No.'

'But you said…'

'Aye. They flame hot but so what. They only flame when they feel lik' it. Sometimes they do and sometimes they don't. All depends. So ye'll be flyin' up there, beggin' yon dragon to flame and next thing, bam, thay got ye and ye's crispy fried like this.' Boy held up a chicken thigh.

'So you don't know how to make them flame on demand.'

'Nay. Ne'er seen it done. It's nae possible.'

'They did it.'

'Aye, but them's not us, is them?'

'You're right,' said Plob with a sigh. 'Them is not us. But it's a start. Let's get some sleep. Tomorrow we'll get some of these crystals that you're talking about and start again.'

The two trudged back to Plob's dwellings, heavy of heart and foot and dripping with chicken grease.

Chapter 10

Not everybody knows this but; moving dragons from one reality to the next does really bad things to the space-time continuum. There are a number of reasons for this but for the purposes of this novel let us assume that we don't really care about the whys. Well…okay, quickly now - just to clarify things.

When the Vagoths go from their universe to the next they do not do so instantaneously, however, they do go from place to place very, very (keep saying very for about another half an hour) quickly. Unbelievably massive distances are travelled at speed approaching the speed of light. At these speeds something called Time Dilation occurs. In other words, time goes by slower the faster that you are moving. Now, if this were allowed to happen to the Vagoths then, when they got home everybody would be...like…umm…a thousand years older than them. So - to negate this effect (theory by Einstein, by the way. Very bright man. Odd hair, dubious hygiene. When he died a Dr. Harvey stole his brain and put it in a pickle jar and kept it for forty three years - true story…I promise), anyway…to negate this, Typhon's spell took this extra time and dumped it randomly into the cosmos. Now - time is very (again many, many verys) very heavy. So heavy, in fact, that this much of it will create a black hole. This is not a problem specifically, unless, of course, you are being dragged into said black hole. Still - it shows a complete lack of caring and a general disregard for the universe on the whole. Typical Typhonic behaviour.

Unfortunately for captain Chole Bhature, his space ship, the Paratha, was at this very moment being dragged into a black hole that was there due to Typhon's random time dumping.

Klaxons blared, lights flashed red and computer generated voices warned warnings of consequences most dire.

Captain Bhature pressed the intercom button and leant forwards. 'Engineering, where is Subji?'

'He's crossing the wefts, captain. He thinks that we may get more output from the woof drives if he gets it right.'

'Tell him I need more power.'

'Captain, it's Subji here. I'm pushing her harder than defunct merchandise at a summer sale. She'll break up if I push her any harder.'

'We have no choice, Subji. I want you to go to woof speed nine.'

'Okydoky, captain. But I'm warning you of consequences most dire.'

'Too late, Subji, the computers have already done so.'

The ship rocked violently from side to side. Diodes blinked on and off, crewmen staggered from side to side and sparks flew from monitors.

'Damage report mister Roti.'

'Shields are down to ten percent, captain. If this continues we're going to have to shut the engines down and go onto Urge power.'

'If we do that, mister Roti, we'll be dragged into that black hole and the pudding will definitely turn to poo. Give me woof factor ten.'

But the gravitational pull of a black hole is

somewhere around the same as the pull of one thousand million million Saturn V space rockets and, as a result, woof factor ten or not, it was less than a minute before the Paratha class A fully-armoured space ship passed the event horizon and was sucked in.

And captain Chole Bhature was entirely correct, because the proof of the pudding is in the eating and this pudding had most definitely become decidedly unpalatable.

The Vagoths arrived again at a little before dusk. The light in the air was thin and grey, and partial cloud cover hid them from view until they were directly over the city of Maudlin.

There were three fighter dragons and four two-headed Belend bomber dragons. The bomber dragons were massive beasts that needed two flyers to control them.

The heavies struck first, spitting out huge slow burning balls of red flame that spun into the city and crashed through buildings, setting fire to all in their paths.

The bowmen and crossbowmen that had been posted around the high points of the city immediately fired back and scores of arrows and bolts filled the skies like swarms of evil, iron-tipped insects. But the dragons flew high and fast and their thick scaly skin caused most of their arrows to bounce off. The odd few missiles that struck hard enough barely penetrated the skin deeply enough to do aught else but hang there like feathered earrings. More decorative than damaging.

In the streets below, fire fighters scurried along the streets carrying buckets of water to douse the plethora of blazes. Then the fighters dropped down, strafing the streets with fast-moving white-hot balls of plasma.

Biggest ran out into the middle of the street, took careful aim with a crossbow, and fired. The bolt bounced harmlessly off the fighter's scales. With a bellow of rage the towering trogre grabbed a pawful of his remaining bolts and threw them as hard as he could at the next dragon.

The bundle of ten quarrels powered through the air with many times more force than mere wood and string could impart. They spread as they flew and the dragon cruised straight into them. Seven or eight of the steel tipped missiles buried themselves deep in the dragon's flesh.

With a high-pitched screech the beast tumbled to the ground, throwing its flyer high into the air and straight into a burning building.

'Yee-hah, you motherless sons of dogs of the female persuasion,' Biggest shouted. 'Eat steel and die. Waits 'till I brings my brothers here, youse is all going to be in deep faeces.'

The rest of the dragons peeled away, climbed quickly into the smoke filled sky. And disappeared.

In the star cruiser, Paratha - time stretched. I mean really stretched. Until it was as thin as a rubber band and as long as forever. Then, because time prefers to exist as an all-encompassing four-dimensional continuum as opposed to a three-dimensional lateral extension, it snapped back.

This resulted in captain Chole Bhature and the rest of the crew of the Paratha all screaming, 'Shiiiiiiiiiiiiiiiiiiiiiiiiiiiiiiiiiiiiiiiiiiiiiiiiiiiiiiiiiittttttttttttttttttttttt tttttttttttttttttt that hurt like buggery,' or some similarly vociferate expletive.

And the Paratha, a class A starship, appeared,

without warning, in the night skies of a hereto uncharted planet in the UDFj-39546284 galaxy. Well, one says uncharted, it had been charted, just not on a star chart. There is no will nor way to chart your relative position in space when you have no space to travel, you tend to simply make a map and assume that you are all…well…there. So - when the mapmakers of Maudlin city had drawn their maps, complete with 'there be dragons' pictures, they had no idea that they were even in the UDFj-39546284 galaxy.

Similarly, the star-charters of the planet Aloo-Matar had no idea that the city of Maudlin was on the planet that was fourth from the sun in the three hundredth solar system from the left in the UDFj-39546284 galaxy.

As a result of this, captain Chole Bhature had no idea that he had appeared in the atmosphere some twenty miles South of the city of Maudlin that was presently under attack by dragons.

He also had no idea that his life, and that of his crew, was about to become the benchmark example of the old adage - 'They went from the frying pan into the fire.'

Nim touched down on the side of the craggy mountain and Plob and Boy climbed down from his back and stretched and stamped and made general stiff-from-long-journey sounds.

Boy pointed at the yawning mouth of a cave about one hundred feet away. 'We'll find all the crystals that we need in there,' he said.

They trudged over to the entrance, both carrying picks and spades and a gross of sisal sacks.

When they got to the cave, Plob conjured up a light spell in the form of a glittering blue ball that danced ahead of them wherever they walked. He did this because Boy had warned him that you couldn't carry flaming torches into caves that held Natrium. Well, strictly speaking that statement wasn't true, you could actually carry flaming torches into a Natrium cave - you simply couldn't carry them out again as a result of being dead. And burnt to a crisp. And dead. (I know - I said dead twice, I'm making a point here). So, blue flickery light it was then.

They walked into the depths of the cave for a while.

'Ye know,' said Boy. 'In th' auld days men used tae carry a chicken wi' thaim whin thay mined.'

'I've heard of that,' answered Plob. 'It was to warn them if there was gas.'

Boy looked at him as if he were mad. 'Na, 'twas fur whin thay git hungry. Thay wid scoff th' chicken.'

'Oh, well maybe the chicken gave them gas.'

'Aye, maybe. A'm hungert.'

'You're always hungry.'

'Tha's true. We're here, look.' Boy pointed up at the roof of the cave. It was covered in crystals of what looked like ice. 'We just chip yon crystals away and pat thaim in the sacks and Robert's your mother's bother.'

The two of them chipped and hacked and shovelled for about half an hour and then dragged the full sacks back to the dragon and strapped them to the saddle.

Boy pointed at something in the undergrowth. 'Look ower thare, tis a talking-fox.'

'What do you mean, a talking fox?'

'Weel, it didna reely talk, but when it barks it sounds jus' lik' it's saying Hello. Come, we'll sneak up reel quite on it and I'll show ye.'

They got down on their hands and knees and

snuck forward.

Chapter 11

All things considered, the ship and its crew had come through the black hole remarkably well. The woof drives were toast but the Urge drive was still intact and all of the shields and weapons systems seemed to be functioning.

'Captain,' said mister Roti. 'I have taken a sample of the atmosphere and it seems compatible to our own. There are large deposits of water and enough raw materials to effect repairs of the woof drive.'

Captain Bhature looked at the monitor and took in the vista. A mountainous terrain, green and verdant with what looked like massive flowered trees and broad bladed bushes. 'Any signs of life?'

'Plenty, captain. The sensors are giving us multiple readings but we haven't seen any as yet.'

The captain stood up. 'Right, let's ready a landing party. I will lead, mister Roti, you, crewman Daal, crewman Masala and crewman Pickle will come with.'

The captain strode from the bridge, pushing aside the beaded curtain that led to the hangers. The rest of the landing party followed.

The five of them climbed into the eight seat, samoosa class, landing craft, the hanger doors opened, the captain fired up the thrusters and took them down to the surface of the unknown planet.

The ship shuddered to the ground with thrusters flaming and landing gear whining. The landing ramp was lowered and the squad walked out.

The captain led the way. 'Set all weapons to "Hurt-like-buggery" gentlemen. We don't know what's out there.'

'I'm sorry, captain,' said crewman Daal. 'I've been issued with one of the new emoto-guns. It doesn't have the old "hurt-like-buggery" setting.'

'What's it got?'

'Umm…hold on, the writing's pretty small. It looks like…angst, then there's suspicion, full-blown paranoia, guilt (levels 1 all the way up to Jewish-son-who-didn't-become-a-doctor) and, finally, existential crisis.

'Put it on guilt level 2, we don't want to kill anyone.'

'Done.'

'Let's go.'

The team strode down the ramp, boldly going where no Aloo-Matarian had ever gone before.

The thick grass came up to their armpits and gorse-like bushes towered above them, their massive purple flowers throwing out a sweet pungent scent.

Then, without warning, a gigantic furred animal appeared from behind a bush. It stood as high as a three-story building and when it pulled its lips back it bared canines that were longer than the captain's arms. Its mouth yawed wide as it pushed towards them, its breath stank of rotting meat and something feral.

'Stand fast, gentlemen,' commanded the captain. 'Don't run.'

The creature stared at them, sniffed and…

'Hellooo,' it said. And again, 'hellooooo.'

'What the…is this creature greeting us,' asked the captain.

'Hello.'

'It appears so,' said crewman Pickle. 'Hello,

creature.'

The massive creature pushed forward, picked Pickle up in its huge maw, chewed twice, and swallowed.

'Fire,' shouted the captain.

Weapons filled the air with the fizz and crackle of energy bolts and puffs of smoke drifted off the creatures fur. But apart from the smell of burning fur the weapons seemed to have no real effect on the goliath.

Then, seemingly from nowhere, a boot the size of a house, whistled through the air and struck the animal in the chest, throwing it over the bush to go yowling on its way. The crew looked up to see a humongous face drift into view, blocking out the sun.

'Look here,' the face bellowed. 'A bunch of wee folks.'

The captain aimed his weapon and pulled off a shot. A bolt of energy hit the face on its nose.

'Ouch,' exclaimed the face. 'That hurt, stop it or ah'll stomp on ye, ye wee bogshites.'

Another face loomed over them. 'Hello, small folk,' greeted the new face. 'Are you Brownies?'

The captain shook his head, not trusting his voice to work correctly in the presence of these giants.

'Leprechauns?'

The captain risked a 'No.'

'Sprite, nymph, pixie, kobold, fairy?'

'No, we are Aloo-Matarians from the planet Aloo-Matar.'

'Why are you so small?'

'We're not,' answered the captain. 'You're big.'

'Same thing.'

No, not at all. I have travelled the seven galaxies and met over two thousand types of sentient beings and none of them have been as gigantonormouse as you. Therefore I put it to you that you are the freakishly sized ones and not us.'

Plob shrugged. 'Whatever. What are you doing here?'

'We are on a five-year mission to explore strange new worlds, to seek out new life and new civilizations and to boldly go where no Aloo-Martarian has gone before.'

'Oh, cool,' said the second head. 'Can we help?'

There was a brief conflab between the miniature Matarians.

The captain nodded. 'Yes please. We appear to be lost.'

'How did you get here?' Asked Plob.

Captain Bhature pointed skywards at the glittering silver space ship. Both Boy and Plob stared for a while.

'Is it held there by magic?' Asked the young magician.

'No,' answered the captain. 'It's held up by Urge power. We were propelled here via a black hole and, as a result, we know not where we are.'

'A black hole?'

'Yes.'

Oh,' said Plob. 'Black magic.'

The captain didn't reply but he did communicate, *sotto voce*, with his crew. 'By the seven gods of Boogahari, where are we, the dark ages? The next thing this giant moron will be asking us is if we've seem any dragons on our travels.'

'Tell you what,' said Plob. 'Why don't you and your magic air ship follow me and my dragon back to our home and we'll see if we can help.'

The crew turned as one and saw the biggest living creature that they had ever set eyes on before. Nim puffed out a lazy billow of sooty flame.

'Well,' said the captain. 'Don't I feel like the asshole?'

Chapter 12

Typhon wasn't happy with the salute. Or the national flag. The Vagoth salute was a little too Simon-says; put your hands in the air. It lacked…gravitas.

He had tried adding to it in order to give it more substance. To the "Hey-oop, Typhon" he had added "All knowing and extremely well respected". But the final thing was far too unwieldy. It lacked snap.

And as for the flag, the Bumsenfaust, a black mailed fist in a white circle on red with a lightning bolt on either side. To be perfectly honest it came across very, well, the word "fisting" sprang to mind. So Typhon had added many more lightning bolts and a second fist. However, this had resulted in something that looked like a BOGOF, Buy One Get One Free, sex-toy advert.

Then Herr Gooballs had made a suggestion. More is less. So Typhon had cut the salute down to the words "Hey All" and, instead of raising two hands had used only the right one. Then he had cut the fist from the flag and done a little redesigning.

Now before him were, once again, arrayed the massed Vagoth troops. They had been instructed on the new salute and the new flag stood, furled, behind him.

Typhon moved to the front of the balcony and waved at the troops.

They responded with the salute, right arms and open palms shooting into the air. Somehow in the instructing they had got the call slightly wrong but to the untutored ear it sounded so similar as to be identical.

'Heil, Typhon. Heil, Typhon. Heil, Typhon.'

Behind the big T the flag was unfurled, the two black SS bolts in a white circle on red fluttered above him.

And somewhere in the foreverness of eternity a switch went - Click. And the universe shuddered and thought, Oh bugger. Not again.

London was burning.

Overhead more than a thousand German fighters and bombers rained fire down on the capital. Anti aircraft rounds stabbed the night in a frantic attempt to deal out some form of retribution. Lances of light crisscrossed the sky as searchlight operators tried to pinpoint an enemy bomber.

In the city small fires became large fires and fire fighters threw sand onto incendiary bombs and water onto flames.

Smudger, who had been given a day's leave after flying almost two missions a day for ten days, sat on a wingback chair, opposite his mother and father, in the middle of the front garden. The house behind him had been reduced to smoking rubble.

Mother was pouring tea into three unmatched cups.

'So good to see you, son. Sorry about the lack of good crockery and the lack of sugar but, well, as you can see, the house has been blown to bits.'

'Don't be silly, mum. It's simply great to have a nice hot cuppa with you two. So, how have things been, father?'

'Well you know how it is, Smudge old boy, mustn't grumble.'

'I see that you appear to have lost you left arm.'

'Oh, yes. Got blown off this morning. Mum strapped the stump up, didn't want to a make a fuss, don't you know, a lot of our neighbours have gone through worse.'

'Really father? Worse than having their arm blown off?'

'Oh yes, look at mister Johnson there,' he replied, pointing at a body lying on the neighbour's front lawn. 'Got his head blown off this morning and I haven't heard a peep of complaint from him the whole day. Mind you, his wife's a bit of an hysteric, sure that I heard her weepin' this afternoon, disgraceful behaviour.'

Smudger's mother shook her head. 'How embarrassing for you, my dear.'

Father lit his pipe. 'Yes, very. She's probably foreign, don't you know. And you, my boy, how goes the war?'

'The Hun send planes over. We shoot them down. Remember Spotty Parker?'

'Short chap, sideburns, flat nose?'

'Yes that's him. He's gone for a Burton. Took a dive into the channel last week. We never found the body.'

A bomb exploded down the street, shattering windows and throwing bits of brick and shrapnel into the air.

Smudger brushed some dust off his tunic. 'Close one.'

'Not as close as the one got to old Charlie Verrucca last week. One landed on his head, blew him clean to bits. Mind you, still puts in a full days work at the fire station, doesn't grumble. Good chap that.'

'How?'

'What?'

'No - how?'

'Oh, I see. Well, when I say that he puts in a full day I may be…stretching it a bit. He does get in late and goes home a little early on Wednesdays due to…well…being dead I suppose.'

'Good for him,' said mum. 'Some more tea, Smudger?'

'Thank you, mum.'

'There you go. Well, I say tea, it's actually hot water. Tea's finished, love. Sorry.'

'Hot water's fine, mum. It's really nice.'

And it was, because, although he was drinking luke warm water in the middle of a burning city, talking to two elderly people who seemed to have retained only the most tenuous link with sanity - at least he wasn't in the cockpit of a Spitfire expecting, at any moment, to die.

And sometimes that is simply the best that one can hope for.

Chapter 13

Nim coughed. And a ball of blue-white plasma sailed across the field and struck a tree. The unfortunate perennial burst into flames and crumbled to the ground.

Plob and Boy whooped in delight and danced around doing much air-punching and foot-to-foot bouncing and backslapping.

'Well,' said Plob. 'The crystals work.'

'Aye, noo a' that we need tae do is figure oot howfur tae mak' it flame on command.'

Plob rubbed his chin and thought. 'Okay, now bear with me. Nim fires up whenever he coughs or sneezes, right?'

'Aye, ya reet.'

'So, what about pepper? We get a bag of pepper and sprinkle a pinch in Nim's nostrils when we want him to flame and…Bam!'

'Aye, Plob, you might ha' summin.'

'What do you think, captain?' asked Plob of the Aloo-Martarian officer who was hovering next to them on a small anti-grav scooter.

He shrugged. 'Gentlemen, this is so far beyond my area of expertise that I feel unable to comment, save to say, how will you control the said dispersal of the pepper?'

'I don't know, we'll cross that bridge when we get to it. First let's see if the pepper works. Boy, fetch my pack, I've got a few boiled eggs for lunch as well as a shaker of salt and a small packet of pepper.' Boy jogged off. 'I'm sorry that we haven't been of any real help, captain,' continued Plob. 'But, as I explained, we're under attack and I'm under huge pressure to come up with some way of getting our dragons to flame hot and hard and on command.'

'Not a problem, Plob. You have replenished our supplies of food and water and given what information that you are capable of. I must say you have taken the whole visitors-from-another-galaxy thing very much in stride. Does our presence not make you wonder? Do we not make you think of all of the things that we might have seen that you have not? Oh, Plob, I've seen things you people wouldn't believe. Attack ships on fire off the shoulder of Origami. I watched p-beams glitter in the dark near the Brownhäppy Gate. And now…all those moments will be lost in time, like tears in rain, unless we find our way home.'

'Oh, I don't know about that. I've been around a bit,' said Plob who was getting ever so slightly irritated at the captain's smug attitude.

The captain lifted a little eyebrow. 'Really?'

'Yes. I have met the queen of the inner Elven lands; I have supped with Stanley, the son of Death. I have parleyed with the grim reaper himself and have charged into battle alongside the renowned hobby-horsemen of the Hors-Doovrees. Dragons have I ridden and dimensions I have crossed, I have thrice died and come back to life, I know all of the secrets of the Magus Transformation Grimoire and…I have seen Jimmy Hendrix in concert.'

There was a silence for a while. 'I apologise, my giant friend,' said the captain. 'Sometimes your apparent lack of technology brings out the worst in me. That was boorish and condescending.'

Plob smiled. 'Marginally, yes. But no worries.'

Boy came running back with Plob's bag, bits of eggshell clung to his chest. 'Sorry, I scoffed a couple to keep me going.' He handed the bag over.

Plob looked inside, it was full of eggshells and remarkably shy of actual eggs. The salt was also gone but, mercifully, the small twist of pepper was still there.

He grabbed a handful of Natrium and fed it to Nim. Then he sprinkled the pepper onto Nim's huge snout. They all stood back a few steps and waited.

They waited.

Waited.

'Och sod it. Tisn't working,' said Boy.

And then Nim had a sneezing fit.

The world went bazonkers!

It had taken her two days to fly there and the city of Maudlin was not at all what Spice had expected. She had grown up in the hills of Strathbarton in the shadow of the Montclear Mountains. She couldn't remember her parents who died when she was only two years old. She had been brought up by her grandparents who were loving, but were so poor that all of the mice actually left their tiny hut to better themselves by moving in with the church mice. And she had never been to a village of more than twenty houses.

But she had heard much talk of cities. The throngs of people. The paved streets. The noises. The beautiful tall buildings and oil lamps that lit the streets at night.

However, she had just flown above the city for the first time and, instead of beauty she saw destruction. Burnt and broken buildings, empty streets and no streetlights. In fact, someone had even fired an arrow at her. It was of no consequence as it had fallen away long before it had reached her but it was, she thought, less than friendly.

She did one more circuit of the city as she looked for a place to land and then suddenly…her world went bazonkers!

White-hot balls of plasma crackled past her, close enough to feel the heat. She stood up in her stirrups and went into a vertical dive as the air around her boiled with fire. Five, ten, fifteen rounds of destruction sizzled past her. She kicked hard right and barrelled along at treetop level, then jinked hard left. When she glanced over her shoulder she could see that more balls of fire were punching into the air where she had been. It was obvious to her now that she had not been the target, merely in the wrong place at the wrong time.

She slowed Tempest down to barely above stalling and winged her way back to the source of the attack. As she cruised in over the treetops she saw two young men in a field with a dragon. The two men were lying on the ground covering their heads with their hands and the dragon was rubbing its snout with its paws and mewling.

Tempest flared her wings and dropped softly to the ground allowing Spice to dismount. She strode over to the closest man and kicked him in the ribs.

'Ouch!' Shouted Boy 'Pick a windae, yer leavin', who's kicking me 'n' how come?' He jumped up. 'Ah will beat ye senseless ye arsehole. Och, tis a lassie. Hey, Plob, git up thir's a bonny lassie 'ere wi' monstrous boots.'

Plob stood up and looked around in a sheepish fashion. 'Wow, we're not dead.'

'You bloody should be,' shouted Spice. 'What the

hell were you doing?'

Plob looked at her and started to talk. But somewhere between thought and deed his ocular input sent a message to his brain that put the kibosh on his rational thinking process. So, what started out as an explanation of sorts, became a tall girl in tight leather with perfection enhancing breasts, flushed cheeks and full red lips. This resulted in the word 'Sfferkwizle' coming out of his mouth as opposed to anything else of a more rational nature.

'What?' Demanded Spice.

Plob rallied his thoughts and started again just as Spice put both hands on her hips and stared at him. The tight black leather of her jacket stretched across her chest as she put her arms akimbo. And, underneath the jacket things moved and thrust and perked in such a fashion as to, once again, head Plob's thoughts off at the pass.

'Numfagoogal.'

Spice's look softened from one of righteous anger to one of concern. 'Oh hell, I'm sorry,' She leant forward and patted Plob on the shoulder. 'Are you all right?' She glanced at Boy. 'I should thought before I shouted. I didn't realise that he was... umm... special. My name's Spice.'

'He's nae special,' said Boy. 'He's normal.'

'Of course he is.' Said Spice.

'Fnooh.' Said Plob.

Spice patted him on the arm.

The young magician took a deep breath. 'Wow! Sorry about that. My name's Plob and I'm not actually special. Well maybe in some ways but not that one. Please, before you have another complete wobbly let me explain.'

And he did, the Vagoth attacks, getting the dragon to flame, trying pepper to create flame on demand

and finally apologising again for almost blowing Spice out of the sky.

'I see,' said Spice. 'So that's the whole story?'

'Almost,' said Plob. 'I forgot to introduce the captain.' He pointed at captain Bhature who had been hovering behind Boy and had just pulled out. 'Captain, this is Spice. Spice, captain Bhature.'

'Oh, a pixie.'

'No,' said Plob. 'He's actually an interstellar cosmonaut from the Papad galaxy in the North-East spiral and he was brought here via a deformation in space-time called a black hole.'

'Really?'

'Yes.'

'I don't know what you're actually saying.'

'Neither do I.'

'Do you have any spare peat for my dragon, she's hungry.'

'Yes. Lots.'

'Well,' said Spice. 'Let's sort the dragons out and then we need to talk about dragon flame and control thereof.'

They led the dragons to the stable to feed.

Chapter 14

'First you take da arrow,' growled Biggest. 'Den yous dip da pointy end in da pitch. Den yous put it onna table next to all de others. See? Den, when da dragons they come overhead you grabs a handful of arrows.' The Trogre picked up a pawful of around sixty arrows. 'You sticks da pointy ends inna flame until dey is all burning. Den you chucks dem at da dragons. You hit da dragons, dey dies and you have done your job. See?'

Biggest looked around at the group of Trogres standing about him. They were all of his younger brothers as he had sent word for them to come poste haste to the capital in order to help defend the city.

And they had all come; Huge, Large, Great, Massive, Broad and Jock who was so named because his mother ran out of synonyms for Big.

Now Biggest, as the only person (Trogre) to have actually brought down an enemy dragon, was training them to be part of T.A.D.S or the Trogre Air Defence System. Initially Biggest had called it the Controlled Response Air Protection System until Jock, who was considered the intellectual of the family, had pointed out the acronym. Biggest had then changed it to the Command Reaction Attack Preservation Scheme. Jock had vetoed that one as well. After much thought Biggest put forward the name, Seriously Hard Intimidating Trogres.

Jock had called them T.A.D.S and put a final end to the lavatorially influenced acronyms after the other brothers pitched in with the Peoples Offensive Outfit.

Huge raised a paw. 'Why does yous light dem?'

'So's you can see dem in de air,' answered Biggest.

Broad put his paw up- next. 'Who died and made yous da king of da place dat we all are? Why does we have to listen to you?'

Biggest leant forward and clubbed Broad on the side of his head with a massive bunched up paw. 'Dat's why.'

Broad rubbed his head. 'Oh, I unnerstand now. Thanks.'

'No problemo, little bro. Dat's what I'se here for. Okay, Massive, you have a practise throw.'

Massive lumbered over, grabbed a bunch of pitch tipped arrows, thrust them into the torch and then threw them into the air with a grunt of effort. The group of brothers watched the flaming arrows arch through the sky.

'Dat is one impressive throw, brudda of mine,' said Biggest. 'But, as dey say in da classics, what go up and such what. So…I sincerely recommend dat we run.'

The Trogres split like long dogs as the ground around them was peppered with flaming yard-long messengers of death.

After the last burning arrow hit the ground Biggest threaded his way around them back to the table. 'Righty-ho my bro's, Huge, you have a go.'

The whole process was repeated as the next brother took his turn. This time, however, Broad wasn't quite fast enough and one of the flaming arrows punched through his foot. The ensuing laughter from the other brothers lasted for well over a minute.

Witty comment came thick and fast but, as Trogres are known more for their ability to crush heads than to invoke intellectual witticisms, they were all along the lines of, 'hey, yous got a burning foot,' or 'Yous is lucky dat you is such a flame retardant mutha or you'd catch alight.'

After all of the brothers had been given a chance to practice, Biggest assigned them their posts.

'Right, dere is seven of us. I will be a roamin' Trogre dat will help out where de action is heaviest. Da rest of you will be situated at da four corners of da city.'

'But dere six of us,' said Broad. 'And even I know dat dere's more in six than in four.'

'Six sides is a polygon.' Said Giant, apropos of nothing.

'Polly gone where?' Asked Broad.

'Nowhere, polygon is a six sided thing.'

Jock shook his head. 'No, is a hexagon you thinking of. Polygon is just many sides.'

'Shuddup,' said Biggest. 'You all know what I means. You be spread around da ourtskirts of da city. Dats all.'

'And da parrot?' Asked Broad.

'What parrot.'

'Da one dat gone. Polly.'

Biggest punched Broad in the face.

'Oh,' said Broad. 'I unnerstand.'

Spice had shown Plob the dragon-firing bit that her grandfather had designed for her. It fitted over a dragon's head and mouth like a bit and bridal on a horse. The difference being that, instead of working on the lips and roof of the mouth to steer, it was solely used to depress the dragons tongue down to create a mild gag reflex which would, in turn, cause a ball of fire to be ejected from the beasts mouth. In other words, you gave a tug on the reins and - Bam! As opposed to chucking pepper at the beast and randomly spraying the area with fire.

The girl explained that, on a full feed of Natrium crystals, a dragon would be capable of around ten to fifteen shots before it needed to eat and recharge.

Plob had taken the bit to Blean the blacksmith who had made up one to fit Nim's larger head and then the two teenagers had flown away from the city so that Plob could get in a bit of firing practice.

It was proving to be hellishly difficult but, after six shots, Plob had managed to hit a hay bale that they had hung from the top branches of an Oak tree.

They flew back for lunch and refuelled the dragons with more Natrium crystals.

They ate in relative silence since Spice was not used to company and worked on the theory that it was better to stay still and let people *think* that you may be an ignorant mountain hick than to talk and cause people to *know* that you were.

As a result she didn't tell Plob how well he had actually done. She had spent her life with mountain dragon folk and never before had she seen a person pick up the difficult art of dragon firing so quickly. This, combined with his almost uncanny ability to make his dragon perform aerial manoeuvres that were nigh on impossible, made Plob most probably one of the best flyers that she had ever seen. The fact that he was, to all intents and purposes, a rank amateur irked her more than a little. Apart from that, she liked him. He was presentable, well built and polite and he looked at her as if she were the most beautiful thing that he had ever seen.

Her silence caused Plob to assume that, firstly, he was an embarrassingly rubbish shot, so he vowed to himself to try even harder that afternoon. And, secondly, that she had noticed his apparent inability to stop staring at her leather encased bosom, so he vowed to himself that he would...stare in a more subtle fashion for the rest of the day. It wasn't that he didn't want to look Spice in the eyes it was just that, when he did, he found it to be more disturbing than staring at her magnificent front. Chests were chests but Spices dark green eyes frightened him. If he looked for too long he found that his heart started beating like a broken clock and he felt an almost undeniable need to throw himself to his knees and declare undying devotion. He was sure that it was all an infatuation brought on by a surfeit of testosterone combined with long lithe feminine legs and skintight leather, so, until he got over it he would stick to staring at Spice's shirt-puppies instead.

After a short rest they took off for more practise. On their way to the outskirts they came across an unkindness of eight or so ravens flying over the fields. As it was the beginning of the lambing season and Plob knew that the local framers were trying to thin out the raven population, due to attacks on newborn lambs, he decided to use them as target practice.

His first round took out the leading raven and the rest of the unkindness scattered. He jinked left to follow one, fired, hit. Went right, hit. Left again, miss, hit. Climbed, fired. Two at once. The last two spilt up, one going high and the other low. Plob kept straight and level and then pulled Nim into a mini-dive and pull up, firing twice as he did so. Both ravens disappeared in a flash of flame.

Plob punched the air and glanced over at Spice.

But his whoop of excitement jammed in his throat when he saw the look on her face. She pointed back towards the city, took Tempest into a sharp turn and headed back. Plob followed at a distance feeling a little shamefaced.

They landed in the field and Plob slid down from Nim and walked quickly over to the girl. 'Look, Spice, ravens are considered vermin by the locals, it may have seemed a little over the top but I can assure you…'

'Oh, be quiet,' she snapped as she climbed down from her dragon. 'Who cares about a bunch of flying rats. But you,' she walked right up to Plob. 'What you just did up there is impossible. That was beyond skill, it was…' she clenched her hands in front of her face as she groped for words. 'That was…' she gave up, put her arms around Plob's neck and pulled him into a fervent kiss.

Plob was now more puzzled than ever, but the tiny piece of his brain that wasn't going; "Wayhey!!!" knew when to keep quiet.

So he did.

And it was good.

The Vagoths came again that night to sow fiery destruction throughout the city. King Bravad had forbidden either Plob or Spice to go up against them, as he did not want to risk his only two usable dragon fighters. He had a plan for the two teenagers.

Biggest and the T.A.D.S brought down two dragons and wounded another, but all in all it was another night of one-sided war and loss.

Chapter 15

'Captain, we managed to isolate the enemy dragons primal signatures during last night's attack,' said mister Roti, the science officer. 'We have now set the Random Acquisition Data Relays to automatically quantify the expected mass and bearing of the adversarial airborne beings visa-vie their relative placement in both time and space.'

Captain Bhature sifted through the maze of techno-speak and translated. 'You've set the RADAR to track incoming dragons?'

'Yes, captain,' agreed the science officer with a small sniff of disapproval. 'However, it's not that simple. I have also added a temporal length factor with an amplitudinal tramontanian response analysis.'

This one was a little more difficult but eventually... 'You can tell how far away they are and how long it'll take to get here?'

'Yes, sir. Also, crewman Daal has been involved in the process of steeping L-theanine in a balneal of aqua pura in order to facilitate the offering of a calescent potable libation.'

Bhature stared for a while as his brain chewed through the orgy of unnecessary loquaciousness but this one had him cold. 'Science officer Roti.'

'Yes, captain.'

'Could it be that you are removing the urine?'

'Sir?'

'Taking the piss, Roti.'

'No, sir.'

'Well then, pray tell, what the hell did you say that crewman Daal is doing, and no fancy words.'

'Making tea, sir. Would you like a cup?'

'Certainly would, science officer. And get someone to ready my grav-cycle, I need to tell Plob about the RADAR.'

King Bravad had sent messengers to all parts of the kingdom and had called up all and any trained dragons and flyers.

But dragon flying is a rich man's sport and there are few rich men. There are even fewer that would spend their wealth riding around on a two ton, fire breathing death trap.

How many, one might wonder? Well, I'll tell you. Exactly thirty-six excluding Plob and Spice.

The Vagoths had over five hundred.

And why do they have so many may you ask? Once again - I'll give you the real, actual, cosmic reason; Because the forces of Evil shall be legion - and the forces of good shall be...well...thirty-seven.

Sucks doesn't it?

On the plus side, they had many more dragons than flyers. Breeders had, after a little royal persuasion, bulked up the available dragon count to eighty-two, including eleven, rare, huge, double headed, Longcaster dragons that needed at least two flyers each to control them.

King Bravad, who had been a professional soldier before he had become king, glanced around the room of flyers. Rich men and rich men's sons. Public school boys almost to a man. The odd mountain dweller or circus flyer but, on the whole, a club of the lands elite. Heavy on teeth, light on chins, voices that could barely manage a vowel and mouths that hardly opened when talking. Nicknames like 'Sausage', 'Pumpkin,' 'Bunny,' and 'Bumpy,' echoed around the room. 'Toast' became 'taste' and 'book' became 'buk' and 'house' rhymed with 'mice.'

But Bravad had seen these buggers fight before and he knew that they were the hardest, most vicious combatants in the land. More so because they saw war as an honourable sport with rules and etiquette. They believed that war had winners and losers and they played the game to the very limit of their innate superiority and beyond, after all, it would be less than honourable to do otherwise.

Bravad, on the other hand, was a crass professional, so he knew that in war there were only losers and dead people. So he fought to stop the war as quickly as possible as opposed to fighting for honour.

The king drew his sword and rapped it on the table for attention.

'Gentlemen.'

Conversation stopped, teacups were put down, moustaches were stroked, pipes were filled and positions of studied insouciance were adopted.

'Gentlemen,' he repeated. 'I have called you all here today because, as you know, we are at war.'

This statement was greeted with a round of applause, like he had just announced an up coming tennis tournament or sailing regatta.

'The Vagoths have come here from another dimension and are using their dragons to burn us at will. I suspect that this is simply the beginning…a softening up phase, if you would. It shall be up to the people in this room to stop this new enemy.'

Another round of applause. Then someone asked a question. There was nothing so crass as raising a hand or deferentially approaching the king, he simply raised his voice and asked. 'I say, sire, I'm sure that I speak for all of us when I say that we're all jolly keen to have a crack at these fellows but one does feel compelled to ask, how?'

'We will fight them in the air. Dragon on dragon.'

'Well, with all respect, my liege, we'll give it a damn good go but it's likely to be a very short fight, what with our beasts being unable to flame and theirs being more of the fulguratic variety.'

Bravad grinned, in the same way that a wolf does before it attacks. 'Gentlemen, follow me.'

They filed after the king who led them to the royal jousting lists. At the end of the lists was a twenty-foot flagpole with a bale of hay on the top. Bravad guided the noblemen to the stands and bade them wait.

Within a minute or so two dragons appeared over the horizon and bore down on the crowd. They flew wingtip to wingtip and as they drew closer they accelerated into a spectacular series of aerobatic flying. Snap turns, suicidal dives, loops and barrel rolls that brought them above the waiting throng.

The one dragon climbed high above them and the second dragon came thundering over the lists, the massive wings raising clouds of dust as they propelled the two-ton body through the air.

And then, without warning of any sort, the dragon spat a ball of white-hot flame. The fire struck the hay bale causing it, and the top ten-foot of flagpole, to simply disappear.

The dragon rolled into a snap turn and came back down the lists firing as it came, once, twice, three times. The balls of flaming plasma tore up the turf as they exploded on contact.

Then the dragon turned again, flared its wings, dropped gracefully onto the ruined sod and sat down so that Plob could dismount. The second dragon dropped down and landed next to it, also sitting to allow Spice to climb down.

The nobles went wild.

Chapter 16

Typhon had been struggling. He simply could not transport more than six dragons across the divide at a time. So he had called on his pet witch. And a blacker and more midnight hag one would struggle to find. Warts had she aplenty, a nose as long and hooked as a dog's hind leg, hair like hanks of greased yarn and eyes as crossed as a frog in a flytrap.

But when it came to the dark arts there was none darker.

'Blood magik,' she said to the demon lord. 'As I have told you before, true power can only be gained through the sacrifice of sentient beings. If you want to move a greater quantity over the divide then you need blood. Barrels of blood.'

Typhon had tentatively approached Gooballs and explained. He was surprised to find how easily the Vagoth minister accepted the theory.

'That shouldn't be a problem,' he had assured the big T. 'We can use goblins, after all, nobody likes them. How many, twenty, thirty?'

The demon shook his head. 'Oh no, that won't do at all. To create real power we're talking about much, much more.'

'Not a problem,' continued Gooballs. 'A hundred?'

'Umm…you know what, this is my fault,' said Typhon. 'I'm obviously not expressing myself succinctly. I need gobs of them, loads, oodles, plenty, reams, scads slathers, tons, wads.'

'Thousands?'

Typhon smiled. 'Now we're getting close.'

They used the army to round them up. The goblins were housed in the open, like cattle, penned in by barbed wire fences and armed guards with barely enough space to all lie down at the same time.

Now he had to figure out some way to undertake mass sacrifice and blood collection and he would be ready for a full-blooded attack on Plob and his bleeding heart philanthropic friends.

It was the 29th of October 1940, England, United Kingdom. Flight Lieutenant Smudger Smith, flying officer Jonno Johnson, flying officer Belter Bigstone and Polish pilot officer Rufin Kowolsky, were returning from a punitive strike against a German bomber offensive. It had been a good hunt. Between the four of them they had downed nine enemy aircraft, however, they were now perilously low on both fuel and ammunition and were heading home.

'Good one, gentlemen,' said Smudger. 'Proud of you chaps.'

'Stop it, captain,' replied Belter. 'You've got me all blushing like a bride on her wedding night.'

There was general laughter over the R/T.

'No peanut butter for chrysanthemums,' added Rufin. 'It leaves marks on the partridge.'

'Captain.' Belters voice crackled with urgency.

'Roger, Belter.'

'Three o'clock. Angels eighteen. What do you see?'

Smudger shielded his eyes against the setting sun. Suddenly they sprang into view. 'I see trouble. Junkers, Dorniers, Heinkles, Messerschmitts. Maybe three hundred?'

'I concur, captain.'

Smudger thumbed his R/T. 'Sector control, sector control, this is 121 Eagle, come in please.'

'Go ahead, Eagle.'

'Control, please be advised that we confirm three hundred plus bandits coming in over Dover at angels eighteen. Where are our fighters?'

'Radar is down, Eagle. Please reconfirm, three hundred plus bandits.'

'I confirm.'

'We'll try to get the big wing out there as soon as, Eagle. In the meanwhile, we recommend that you attack.'

'We roger that, control. Please be advised that there are only four of us and we are low on ammo and fuel, so not sure how long we can keep these buggers interested. Please send more partners to the dance as quickly as you can. Eagle out.'

'Control out, and good hunting, gentlemen.'

'Well, you heard the man,' said Smudger. 'Let's go, boys.'

'Tally ho.'

'Once more into the breach.'

'The bicycle puts fluff on the peas.'

Chapter 17

Death exists.

I'm not talking about the concept of death. Nor some form of ancient god thereof that has been brought to life by the mass-mind of worship.

For example; other inevitable occurrences, like disease, exist only as a thing that happens. There is no Disease with a capital D as in Death.

There is the concept of love. There are many gods of love. But there is no - Love. No Birth, no Honour, no Happiness and no Wisdom.

There is only Death.

Only Death exists in a solid, non-ethereal, practical way. He puts on robes of darkness every morning, he eats meals, he worries about the state of the universe in general and…he has a child.

Stanley.

The son of Death.

'Black,' thought Stanley. 'Always black. Not even a colour, simply an absence thereof.'

The boy was depressed. People joke about the fact that death is hereditary…but in Stanley's case it literally was. When it came down to it, death was simply natures way of say… 'You're fired.'

And dad would never let him get involved in the family business. In fact, only the night before had been preparing dinner, Stanley was chopping the carrots - dicing with Death, as it were - and he asked his dad if he could maybe do a couple of pick-ups. It was his time to start helping with the whole, ushering of souls thing, he told the father of darkness. He hadn't even bothered to answer.

It's not that it sucked being a teenager…it's just that Stanley had been a teenager for about as long as he could remember. Which is like, forever.

It's not as though it sucked only wearing black, Johnny Cash did well out of it…it's just that, if he tried to wear another colour, red for example, by the time he had pulled the shirt over his head it was black.

It's not as though it sucked waiting to take over the family business…it's just that, when your father is the Alpha and Omega, time without end - well, forever is a long, long time to wait.

And when you put all of these little niggles together…it did suck a bit.

Also - he never met any girls. Well, he did, but they were dead. And the biggest problem with dead people is that they are incredibly boring. Most of them are so shocked to have gone over that they hang around in the processing areas like a bunch of sheep. He supposed that was where the expression, "Dead Boring" came from.

Anyway, Stanley decided to take a walk to the processing rooms and watch the newcomers. He had nothing else to do.

When he was about halfway to the halls he heard an unusual sound. Unusual for the land of the dead, that is. Laughing. Voices raised in excitement. Friendly banter. He walked swiftly over the small hill to see who it was.

Four men. All dressed in similar fashion. Dark blue uniforms, white jumpers, large, fur-lined leather boots, fur-lined leather jackets and some sort of small leather hat or helmet. One was smoking a pipe.

Stanley hurried forward to greet them.

King Bravad had broken up the thirty-six flyers into six wings of six. He then allocated the most experienced in each wing the rank of "Dragon Wingman". He had kept both Plob and Spice out of the general dragon force and had designated them the rank, "Dragon Commander." The rest of the flyers were designated the rank of "Dragonman" and the whole team was top be referred to as the "Dragonflight".

They had spent every waking moment of the last week training, puzzled that they had not been attacked but thankful for the respite. After a gruelling week Plob had told the king that he was relatively happy that they would be able to put up a good show when the Vagoths next came at them. Particularly now that captain Bhature had provided them with an early warning system.

He was wrong.

With Typhon's new Goblin-sacrifice enhanced power he managed to send a much larger flight than ever before.

Fifty Vagoth dragons penetrated Maudlin's airspace at some ten minutes after first light. The attack consisted of twenty heavies and thirty fighters. The Dragonflight took off with fair warning and were in the air to meet them.

It was a massacre. Plob would never forget the screams of dying dragons and men. Dragons turning and climbing and diving and firing. Everywhere, balls of burning plasma flashed through the air. Beasts colliding in midair, riders dropping to their deaths.

His own Dragonmen's fire as dangerous as the enemies as it sprayed randomly around the sky.

He managed to bring down four enemy fliers, Spice managed one. The rest of the Dragonflight knocked down another three for the loss of twenty-six.

In one attack the Dragonflight was as good as finished.

Chapter 18

Once again German bombs rained down on London. Explosions ripped through the capital, levelling buildings and creating fires and dealing out the cards of death in an indiscriminate fashion.

And amongst the wreckages and ruins scurried the heroes that were the citizens of London.

Blean dragged the second body from the burning building just before the thatch roof collapsed. Above he could hear the sounds of the enemy dragons shrieking as they fired, indiscriminately, into the city of Maudlin.

A dragon tumbled from the sky as the T.A.D.S locked onto it and filled it full of arrows. He heard screaming from another burning building and ran in, looking for someone else to save.

Against all of the odds and then some more, the old man in London was completely unscathed. The five hundred pound bomb had landed in the street outside and completely levelled his house…except for the toilet.

And there he sat, pants around his ankles, a telephone book, cut in half, in his right hand in lieu of toilet tissue.

On his face a look of complete bemusement.

'I only pulled the bloody chain,' he kept saying to himself.

'Come on,' shouted Blean, as he rushed through the streets of Maudlin. 'Let's start a bucket chain to put this fire out.'

'I'll help you,' chimed a passer by.

'Sorry,' replied Blean. 'No time for that. I'll do it by myself.'

In the next street a group of newly orphaned children attacked a fallen Vagoth flyer with pitchforks and cudgel, beating and stabbing him to death, looks of stolid concentration on their young, fire streaked, faces.

The ambulance pulled up next to the burning pub. Above the door hung a crooked sign, 'English spoken here…Australian understood.'

A woman lay bleeding on the pavement, thrown there by the bomb blast, her broken leg twisted at an impossible angle underneath her. She was laughing.

'Are you alright, Madam?' Asked the driver, worried that she may be hysterical.

'Oh yes, my good fellow. It's just funny because I think that's the first time I've ever actually been thrown out of a pub.'

And so it was. Across time and space the separate battles raged as, unbeknown, two very different peoples fought two very different enemies that were, actually, the same.

Chapter 19

Plob had fought in battles many times before. He had fought using magic, swords and conventional weapons. He had fought alongside the hobby-horsemen of the Hors-doovrees and British secret agents. He had seen death in many guises and had taken his first life when only fifteen years old. But never before had he been exposed to such wanton destruction. Such a one sided annihilation. And it was his fault.

He had told the king that they were ready. He had assured him. He had filled his fellow dragonmen with confidence. And then he had led them to their deaths.

Now the Dragonflight consisted of him, Spice and ten others. The next enemy attack would finish them.

He heard a low buzzing sound and looked up to see captain Bhature and science officer Roti approaching on their grav-scooters. Both had looks of restrained excitement on their faces.

'Plob,' said the captain. 'I think that we can help. Science officer Roti has been doing extensive research on your dragons and their method of fire production. He has come up with a formula of different crystals that, if fed to them in the correct dosage, will not only triple their fire output, it will also increase heat, speed and explosive capabilities.'

Plob waved him away. 'No point, captain. We're finished. We have no more flyers.'

'I assure you, this could turn things around. They won't have any answer to this magnitude of firepower.'

'So?'

'So get some more flyers.'

'Where?'

The captain shrugged. 'I don't know.'

'Well neither do I,' answered Plob as he stood up and walked away. The teenager wandered aimlessly for a while, wallowing in self-pity and guilt and doubt. Eventually he simply sat down in the middle of a field and did nothing. After a while he heard a noise behind him and he turned top look. It was Biggest.

The Trogre ambled forward and offered Plob a flask. Plob remembered the flask well; it was a magical gift that had been bestowed on the Trogre some while back by master Smegly's master. It contained a never-ending supply of Blutop, a rough sugarcane spirit that could double as a silver polish and a rust preventative. He took a swig and shuddered. Took another. Passed it back.

Biggest squatted down on his haunches. 'So, boy, yous is givin' up?'

'Yep.'

'Jus' like that?'

'What else can I do, Big?'

'Well, for a start, *not* giving up comes to mind. You know, my frien', my daddy used to say to me, "Biggest, you is acting like da most uselesseses piece of poo dat I has ever comed across, I auta beat you to death wiv a big stick or summat."'

'Oh,' acknowledged Plob. 'So?'

'So, nuttin'. Youse my frien' so I's not gonna talk to you in dat less dan respectful way.'

The teenager thought for a while. 'So what you're

saying is; I'm acting like a useless piece of poo?'

Biggest shrugged. 'I didn't say dat. I intimated it through da subtle use of homily and moralising discourse regarding my *paterfamilias* and what he did say to me when I was feeling down.'

'So, in this scenario, I'm the useless piece of poo.'

'Acting like,' said Biggest. 'Acting like one.'

'So what do you advise I do?'

'O dunno, in da scheme of things at da moment I is just a simple weapons system for shooting down dragons. You, on da udder hand, is a Dragon Commander and a magician, but I can say dis; doing anytin is betta dan doing sod all.'

Plob flushed up with shame. People had died and he had decided to wallow in self-pity instead of doing anything. Instead of even trying to do anything. He stood up. 'Thanks, Big. I've got things to do.'

'Dat you do, my young fren'. Dat you do.'

The massive Trogre sat alone for a while and drank from his magical flask. He was a good boy, dat Plob, he thought. Especially for a human.

Biggest didn't blame the teenager for becoming a little confused, after all, it must be difficult to think properly when you spent the majority of your life with your brains less than three feet from your bum.

The new dragon fire formula that Roti had formulated consisted of a blend of Natrium, Brimstone, Charcoal, Iron filings and Grain alcohol.

Boy mixed up a batch and fed it to one of the riderless dragons. Then they watched and waited. After ten minutes the dragon belched lightly, producing a small ball of flame and then…the beast simply exploded.

The explosion itself was large enough to leave a sizable crater in the field and quick action was needed to douse the fires that had started on the dragon pens from bits of burning dragon.

Roti did some quick recalculations. 'Right. I see what went wrong.' He wrote frantically on a small piece of paper which he handed to Boy. 'That'll fix it.'

Boy stood with a look of horror on his face. 'Gods, how am I goin ta stick the poor brute back together wa' this?' He waved the tiny piece of paper in the air.

Roti throttled back frantically on his IQ, knocking about one hundred points off so that he could figure out what Boy was talking about. 'No, Boy. It's the new formula mix. The dragon's gone, nothing that we can do about it. Mix up another batch of crystals according to the weights on that piece of paper and let's try again.'

Boy mixed up another batch. Plob led another dragon in. It fed. They waited, crouched behind any cover that they could find. After twenty minutes all seemed safe.

Plob told boy to saddle the dragon and he did so, pulling the stomach cinch in gingerly as he did.

'What's its name?' Asked Plob.

'Petronus.'

The teenage magician climbed aboard. 'Right, Petronus. Let's fly around a bit and see what we got.'

He took the beast up to treetop level and pulled a couple of slow, easy turns. Then he climbed high, did a barrel roll and then dived. The dragon responded perfectly.

'Right, mister dragon. Let's get serious.' He lined up with a tree at the end of the landing field. Aimed about halfway and…squeezed the firing reins.

Three white-hot balls of plasma shot from Petronus' maw in under a second. The fire travelled at least four times quicker than any that Plob had seen before. When the plasma stuck the tree it didn't merely burn, it literally exploded into ignition. One moment it was there, the next, a smoking stump of smouldering ash.

Plob pulled the dragon into a sharp right turn and fired again, a long pull on the reins. The dragon discharged a massive volley of flaming balls. A holocaust of fire ripped through the trees, sap exploded in the heat and leaves crackled to nothing in seconds. He pulled up and picked a target further away, some four hundred yards. He lined up, fired. Another trio of flaming rounds of plasma scorched through the air and struck their target.

Plob weaved back and forth, firing and firing again until, when he pulled the reins, the dragon merely hiccupped and discharged a small puff of smoke.

He guided Petronus back to ground, his heart filled with elation.

Forty-three rounds. Forty-bloody-buggery-three rounds of white hot, balls to the wall, destruction.

Maybe there were only twelve Dragonmen left but next time, Plob vowed to himself, they would take a few more enemy with them before they cashed in and went to the other side.

Chapter 20

Smudger shook his Zippo and then tried, once again, to light his pipe but it was obviously out of fuel.

'Here,' said Stanley. 'Let me.' He snapped his fingers and the bowl of tobacco started to smoulder.

Smudger nodded his thanks and puffed the pipe into life. 'So,' he said. 'We're dead.'

Stanley nodded. 'Afraid so.'

'Darn it. Must say, can't remember much. We attacked that bunch of Krauts, I think I ran out of ammo…or fuel…or both. Next thing…burning…then here. What about you chaps?'

Jonno and Belter shrugged. 'Pretty much the same, captain,' said Belter.

'Friction causes soap bubbles,' agreed Rufin with a smile.

'I don't suppose that we could…well…be sent back?' Asked Smudger. 'It's just that, we're at war, you see, and I'm pretty sure that we're the good guys.'

Stanley shook his head. 'Sorry, chaps. Not much chance of that on account of being, well, dead.'

'Deceased,' said Smudger. 'Who would have thought?'

'Bereft of life,' added Belter.

'Gone for a Burton,' sighed Jonno.

'Bowling made the sheets mouldy,' stated Rufin. 'We rest in peace.'

Smudger grinned. 'You know, that one almost made sense, Rufin old chap.'

Rufin smiled back. 'Yes. The trowel grows cold.'

'Here comes my father,' said Plob. 'You're welcome to ask him but, I'm warning you, he's really big on dead is dead is dead, so I wouldn't hold much hope.'

Death strode up to the group and then stopped and looked. Without conscious thought the pilots all stood to attention and saluted while Death added and subtracted and weighed what was left of their souls.

Smudger stepped forward and offered his hand. 'Pleased to meet you, sir. I'm flight lieutenant Samuel Smith and these are my chaps.'

Death took Smudger's hand. And it was as cold as ice and as hot as Hades. And Samuel looked into his eyes and back at him stared the abyss. Abbadon and Gehenna. Domdaniel, Jahannan and Sheol. One hundred million, million souls. Pain and joy and agony and ecstasy. Emotion without end.

And he fell to his knees and begged forgiveness for all that he had done and not done. For he was in the presence of He Who Rides the Pale Horse and everything else counted for naught.

'Rise, lieutenant Smith. You have done little evil in your life. And anyway, it is not for me to judge you. I am merely the custodian of life. I neither give it nor do I take it away.'

'Sir, I ask that you allow my men and me to return so that we may carry on the fight. I am sure that I speak for all when I say that we would gladly return afterward, we merely ask a boon of some borrowed time.'

'I have watched your war. Many times. Your presence will not make a substantial difference to the outcome. You have all done your work well. You should feel proud.'

'Sir, may I ask…do we win the war?'

Death stood for a while, his eyes blank. Then he nodded. 'Most times, yes. Not always.'

'What do you mean. Sir? Either we win or we lose.'

'Lieutenant, I could be trite with you and tell you that there are no winners in war. This would be a statement of truth, however, I am sure that is not what you mean. I do not see things in the same linear fashion as you do. I see all...I know all. Everything that has been, that is being and that will be. And I see it all at the same time.

'Wow,' said Smudger. 'That must be very confusing.'

Death gave a glimmer of a smile. 'Flight lieutenant, you have no idea. Even a simple chore like making tea becomes an almost Sisyphean task when attempted in n-dimensional space. I am sorry but I cannot help you and your men, however, you are welcome to stay in my domain as long as you want, whatever you wish for, within reason, will be made available and we shall talk at another time about what you will all do next.'

Death turned and strode away.

Stanley clicked his fingers and a table appeared with four wingback chairs arrayed around it. Another click and four crystal tumblers appeared on the table next to a bottle of fifteen-year-old Talisker single malt whisky and a bottle of Wyborowa wodka.

Rufin picked up the bottle and his eyes misted with tears. '*Dziękują mały śmierć. Ten przypomina mnie mojego domowy,*' he said to Stanley.

'*To jest przyjemnością,*' answered Stanley. 'Gentlemen, I shall leave you to your musings. If you want anything else simply click your fingers and I will come.'

Rufin turned to the rest of the group and held up the wodka bottle. 'Yellow desk here husband,' he said and poured himself a tumbler full. He saluted the others and then downed it in one.

Herr Martin Boredman was a bored man. He sat upright in his large, goose feather mattress bed chewing tobacco and spitting into a golden spittoon. Next to him lay the lithe, almost hairless body of a young man, perhaps eighteen perhaps a little younger.

The new Fuhrer had put Boredman in charge of the Goblin storage camps where all of the goblins were kept in readiness for the mass sacrifices that were needed in order to transport the Vagoth dragon fleet across the divide.

As well as simply storing, the wrenched creatures were being used for forced labour, making weapons, dragon tack and so forth. Most of them were very gifted craftsmen and the goods that they produced were superlative.

He climbed out of bed and wandered over to the window of his four-story mansion that overlooked the storage pens and workhouses. He spat a gobbet of tobacco juice over the balcony and then picked up his cross bow, putting it on his shoulders and twisting from side to side to limber up.

With a grunt of effort he pulled back the cocking lever, inserted a quarrel, rested on the balustrade and aimed at one of the goblins sweeping up the quadrangle. Slowly he squeezed the trigger. The bolt went high and right.

He reloaded, adjusted the sites and lined up again.

As he was pulling the trigger the young man, who had climbed out of bed to join him, smacked him on the left buttock. Boredman jerked upright causing the bolt to bounce off the outside lamp post, hit the next door buildings wall, ricochet up against the steel guttering and come careening back to plunge full length into his right thigh.

He fell to the floor thrashing around and screaming like a banshee. His lover ran around in tight circles, flapping his hands and also screaming blue murder because he knew that, as soon as Boredman recovered, things were going to go very badly for him.

Typhon didn't bother to knock. Supreme commanders did not knock, they simply strode in. And anyway, he had been invited for drinks and eats by Herr Gooballs.

It was the first time that he had been in Gooballs's quarters and the room was…odd. At first it was difficult to put your finger (talon) on what it was and only when the big T sat down in a chair did he figure it out. The entire room, window and all was cunningly crafted to just over one half scale. The glasses of ready cocktails, the plates, even the snacks were half size. It made one feel out of perspective with oneself and caused ones eyes to water and ones brains to flicker back and forth on constant double take mode.

Typhon could hear singing coming from another room, he grabbed a couple of drinks and wandered over. The door was open and there, sitting in a half sized bath, covered in bubbles, was the minister of propaganda, Herr Gooballs.

'Ah, mine Fuhrer, welcome. I was just sitting in the bath you know. The hot water relaxes me. So…here I am…just sitting in my normal sized bath that any normal sized person would sit in. See, I even have normal sized soaps.' Gooballs held up a scale replica of a full sized bat of soap. 'And shampoo bottle. See, all normal sized, just like me.'

Typhon was a demon and, as such, was not fully familiar with human bathing rituals. For all that he knew it was normal to receive guests in the bath. He did wonder what all of the bubbles were for. Soap, he had seen before. But shampoo baffled him.

'You have shampoo?' He asked.

Herr Gooballs picked up a small bottle. 'Yes, here. Many normal sized bottles of shampoo.'

'Why?' Asked Typhon.

Gooballs looked puzzled. 'Umm…for the normal reasons, I suppose.'

'I see. But why *sham*poo – can you not afford real poo?'

Gooballs thought for a while but the non sequitur floored him so he reverted to playing the host.

He stood up out of the bath and walked through to the sitting room, ushering Typhon before him. This wasn't as awkward a moment as one might think because Herr Gooballs was actually fully clothed in his formal Vagoth attire. Black, silver trimmed tunic and trousers with deaths head badge and black cap with the rampant Bumsenfaust mailed fist sticking out the front like an armoured phallus.

He picked up a plate of crackers mounded high with caviar and offered them to his Fuhrer, but soapy water drained had down his arm and puddled the plate turning the expensive Hors d'oeuvre into a mush of detergent, water, biscuit and fish eggs.

Gooballs simply dropped the plate on the floor and helped himself to a drink.

Typhon grabbed another cocktail and downed it in one. 'Don't you have any decent sized tumblers?' He asked. 'Something that I can mix a proper sized drink in as opposed to these bloody thimbles.'

Gooballs eyes glassed over. 'These are decent sized.'

'No,' said Typhon. 'They're tiny. Like you. Now get me a proper receptacle and fill it with booze.'

Gooballs's left eye twitched frantically and the colour drained from his face. 'I'm sure that I don't know what you mean Herr Typhon.'

The big T unfurled his wings. 'Listen to me, you miniature cripple. I am exhausted. Do you have any idea how much energy it takes to send dragons across the divide? I don't have time to play dollies with you and your scaled down accoutrements. Now. Did you ask me here for a reason or did you simply want to show me how "normal sized" you are?'

Gooballs held up his glass. 'S'normal.'

'God's, you are pathetic,' said Typhon as he strode from the room. 'And weird, I mean who keeps bottles of fake faeces in their bathroom. Bloody sham poo…makes me sick.'

The minister of propaganda for the Vagoth Empire burst into tears and rushed through to his bedroom, slamming the door behind him.

Herr Gobling, Chief of the Vagoth flying corps, strolled slowly down the ranks of flyers, inspecting them, chatting with the odd one and generally being imperious.

Next to him walked his second in command, count Rye Beena.

'My dear count,' said Gobling. 'I have had an idea that will bring even greater glory to out beloved flying corps. I aim to show our enemies that we relish the prospect of battle, we court danger, we shall run up the flag and brazenly shout our presence to all.'

'Yes, Herr Gobling?' Enquired the count, politely.

'Yes, indeed, my dear count. I propose, prepare

yourself, that we paint our dragons in primary colours.'

They took a few more steps. Count Rye Beena's face was a picture of discombobulation. 'I'm not sure that I understand, my glorious leader.'

'You know, slap some red and green and blue paint on them. Make them stand out.'

'But Herr Gobling...umm...the dragon's natural colours are already red and green and blue...also black ones and yellow ones.'

'So,' said Gobling. 'Are you the sort of man to let such a simple thing prevent you carrying out my wishes? Are you, count Beena, are you that sort of man?'

'No, my leader, I am not that sort of man. I...umm... we can paint the...umm.'

'Gobling stopped walking. 'Dammit, man. Do I have to do all of the thinking around here? We'll paint the red ones blue...the green ones red...and the black ones yellow. Simple.'

'What about the yellow ones?'

'They can stay,' said Gobling. 'No wait...paint them red.'

'The same as the green ones?'

'No, idiot, the same as the blue ones.'

'But, my esteemed leader, we haven't actually mentioned the blue ones yet.'

'Oh - well paint them...umm...yellow.'

'Like the black ones?' Asked count Beena.

'No - like the yellow.'

'I thought they were black.'

'No they were...red? No, no...green. Look - just paint the dragons different colours or so help me I'll send you to the Russian front.'

'Yes, my leader.'

The two walked for a while.

'Where is the Russian front, my supreme leader?'

Gobling thought for a while. 'You know, I'm not sure. I have no idea why I said that.'

They walked for a while longer.

'I shall call it, "Gobling's Flying Circus."'

'Nice one, my leader. Got a good ring to it.'

'Yes,' agreed the fat megalomaniac dressed in baby blue. 'I thought so.'

Herr Boredman hobbled along; he was carrying his crossbow and leaning on a stick, his thigh heavily strapped from that morning's accident. The young spanker of Boredman's bare bottom had been sent packing for his blunder. In a suitcase. In fact, several suitcases to various different destinations.

The camp secretary, corporal Kountalot, walked beside him. Boredman was on a camp tour, inspecting the workers, dealing out discipline and generally taking his bad mood out on innocents.

They came to a table where a young goblin was frantically putting parts together. Boredman picked one up.

'What is this?' He asked the goblin.

The goblin wound it up and placed it on the tabletop. It wobbled around in a random fashion. Every now and then a small brass bell would spring out of the side, ring twice and then retract.

'Hmm, I see. And what is it?' Boredman asked again.

'If it please your honour. It's a widget.'

'Widget?'

'Yes, sir. A genuine one.'

'What does it do?'

'Well, you see, sir, a widget is a general term for an unspecified device. For example, an economist might discuss the marginal cost of manufacturing a widget. The thing is, sir, that the expression was used so often that people began to actually demand widgets. We are the worlds largest widget manufacturer.'

Are you a good widget maker?'

'Yes, sir.'

Boredman pulled out a watch on a chain. 'Make one.'

The goblin worked swiftly, hammering, screwing and filing. Within a couple of minutes he had put together a genuine widget. He placed it on the table.

'Very good,' said Boredman. 'And very fast as well. A little over two minutes. Excellent. So, tell me, goblin, if you can make one every two minutes and you have been here since the morning why are there are only…' he counted… 'One hundred and five in the box instead of one hundred and seven?'

The goblin cringed back. 'I don't know, your excellency.'

'I am afraid that is not good enough.' Boredman raised his cross bow and pulled the trigger.

The bolt missed the goblin, struck the metal-press on the other side of the table, bounced upwards, glanced off the roof and buzzed earthwards to bury itself in Boredman's other leg.

Mister bushy eyebrows fell to the floor screaming for the second time that day.

'Why!' He screamed at the top of his voice. 'Why me?' He started to beat the floor with both hands like a child in extremis. 'Mommy. Mommy, why didn't you love me? I was a good boy. I rubbed your feet. I washed your back. I did all those things that only special sons do to their mommies. Why am I being punished?' He stuffed his fist into his mouth and bit down hard. Blood poured down his chin and he looked at the floor in horror to see that he had actually bitten the end of his index finger off.

Mercifully, he passed out before he could do any more damage to himself.

Chapter 21

Plob and Spice had spent every waking moment training with the remaining ten members of the Dragonflight. But there is a limit to how much you can improve in a few days no matter how hard you try.

One thing was obvious, though. That was, the weaker flyers had been taken out in the initial disastrous encounter. The remaining ten were, to a man, hard as hell, fly by the seat of your pants, hotdoggers and, with their new improved firepower, Plob reckoned that the Vagoths were in for a surprise. He didn't fool himself, in that he did not let the thought of coming through the next encounter alive cross his mind.

The Dragonflight had their pitched tents near to the dragon stables so as to be as close as possible when the call came. Plob and Spice had pitched their tents away from the others on the other side of the landing field.

That evening, after they had eaten and bathed, Plob crawled into his tent, wrapped a fur blanket around him and lay waiting for sleep that would not come, even though he was exhausted.

He heard a sound at the entrance to the tent and looked up to see Spice who slipped in and sat next to him.

'Can't sleep,' she said.

'Me too.'

Spice pulled her tunic up over her head and then raised her legs so that she could wriggle out of her underwear. Plob's breath caught in his chest.

'You now,' she said. Her voice a husky whisper.

Right…we all know what's going to happen next. I'm not going to write about it in graphic detail because; firstly, I tend to get embarrassed doing so and, secondly, maybe I write something that I think is totally normal and everyone is like…eeuuugh, really. What a pervert…or something.

So, this is what I'm going to do. I'll provide a list of words and then you can put together your own bedroom scene thereby relieving me of the responsibility.

Right – let's go: *Moist, Heaving, Flower, Purple, Grinding, Cleave, Forest, Manipulate, Pork Chop, Enormous, Sweat, Sausage, Juice, Poodle, Friction.*

Afterwards they lay together in silence, hands and minds linked together. A lone candle flickered on the small table next to them, playing with the light and creating a world of undecipherable shadow hieroglyphics on the tent walls.

Spice sat up and rummaged through Plob's knapsack. 'Have you got anything to drink?'

'Yep, there's a flask of Blutop, courtesy of Biggest, in there somewhere.'

'Can't find it.'

'Look harder.'

Spice upended the sack and spread Plob's belongings on the floor. 'Ah, there.' She picked up the flask, uncorked it and took a swig. She shuddered and passed it to Plob who also had a mouthful. 'What's this?' Spice asked, holding up a long black feather. 'I mean, I know it's a feather, but why do you keep it?'

'It's a present.'

'From who?'

'You wouldn't believe me.'

'Try.'

'The son of Death.'

Spice laughed. 'I don't believe you.'

So Plob told her. He had met the son of Death around a year ago when he was last fighting against Typhon and his evil minions. The two of them had come quite close friends and, as a parting gift, he had given Plob a feather from Death's pet cockerel and told him that, if he ever needed help, he should simply hold the feather, concentrate on him and he would come.

Spice looked a little sceptical but Plob assured her that he was telling the truth.

'Well then, use it,' she said.

'Why?'

She shook her head. 'You know, my darling. I truly love you but sometimes you are just a little bit thick. Don't you think that we need help? Desperately.'

'Yes,' agreed Plob. 'But I don't see how he could help us.'

'Plob, we might be dead tomorrow. Isn't it worth a try?'

The teenage magician nodded. 'You're right. Pass me the feather.' He held it in his right hand and concentrated.

There was a sound like all of the air being sucked out of a balloon by an asthmatic septuagenarian and suddenly there were three in the tent.

'Hey, Plob, my man. Long time no see,' said Stanley.

Plob gave the son of Death a quick hug.

Stanley turned to Spice. 'Hi. Wow, nice ti…eyes,' he said.

Spice covered herself up with the blanket.

'Sorry,' said Plob. 'I didn't know that it worked like that.'

Science officer Roti did a little jig. A very, very small one. More in his head, than one done overtly by using his actual body. A mind jig, as befitting a science officer.

The captain walked into the laboratory. 'Happy, officer Roti?'

'Yes, indeedy, captain. Look.' He held out a circle of leather, perhaps an inch across. In the middle of it was a tiny black square.

The captain picked it up. 'Sticky.'

'Yes, captain. But only on the one side.'

'So, what is it?'

'It's a dual acceptance articulation response and dissemination mechanism.'

'Science officer, Roti. We've already spoken about this.'

'Sorry, sir. It's a two way radio.'

'So? We've got lots of those.'

'No, sir, not like these. You see, these are designed for the dragonmen. All that they do is stick this to the side of their necks and that's it. The radio works both ways and all received information is transferred, via bone vibration, directly to the inner ear. It should vastly help their capabilities by being able to communicate freely during combat. Plus, we'll be able to monitor them from our bridge. We can use radar during the battle and then radio them with advice.'

'Very clever, mister Roti. What's the battery life on those things?'

'Well, pretty much forever, you see, it involves the use of the degeneracy system whereby, if the energy of different states is the same, the energy level is called degenerate. However, in this 1D system there is no degeneracy. We then combine an eigenfunction of the time-Independent Schrödinger Equation and substitute...'

'Mister Roti. Simplify.'

'Sorry, captain. I can't. It's quantum mechanics, sir.'

'Hmmm...quantum mechanics, I know something about that, something to do with a cat in a box isn't it? You put a cat in a box, along with a hammer and some poison and a radioactive isotope...ummm, I forget exactly how it goes. Anyway - you better keep some bandages on hand because, when the cat gets out, he won't be happy.'

'Yes, sir...that's sort of it. Captain, there is one more thing, take a look at this.' Roti swung the viewer to the electron microscope over to the captain who looked into the eyepiece.

'What am I looking at?'

It's a one hundred thousand times magnification of a sulphur molecule. I was working on increasing the explosive power of the dragon food.'

Captain Bhature looked again. 'So?'

'One hundred thousand times magnification, sir.'

'Officer Roti, for the moment let us pretend that, while you were at university getting a doctorate in molecular science, I was at the naval academy learning how to fly this ship and, as a result, I have no idea what you are going on about.'

'Sorry, sir. It's too big. It shouldn't look like that. That's how it should look under a mere eight thousand times magnification.'

'What does that mean?'

Roti shook his head. 'I'm not one hundred percent sure, captain. I have some theories but haven't tested them yet. All that I can say is…it's wrong. It shouldn't be that big…or maybe, to put it another way - we shouldn't be this small.'

Spice was intimidated by Stanley. She wasn't sure why. He was polite, he had a …dark…sense of humour and he obviously liked Plob.

But if you happened to look him in the eye, even fleetingly, it felt like time had stopped. No…she corrected her thinking, not stopped - slowed down. It had slowed down because, unlike normal people with their three score and ten, these eyes reflected back eons. Lives and deaths beyond counting. A million million rainy Monday mornings staring back at you.

In short - it was intimidating.

'I'm sorry, Plob,' said the descendent of dissolution. 'You know the rules. We've been through this before.'

'I know, but I'm as desperate as a fifty year old virgin. The next time that the Vagoths come in strength I'm dead.'

'You've been dead before.'

'As true as that is, Stanley, it's of little bloody comfort. And, it's not only me. It's all of us. The death of a nation. Do you want that on your conscience?'

Stanley looked up and his eyes crackled with raw power. 'Careful, my friend. I have no conscience, how could I? Also - I am not responsible for the rise and fall of nations. I am merely the son of the ultimate caretaker. So do not bandy with words, you are my friend, you have asked for help. I will do what I can but I must warn you that there is little that I can do.'

Plob held his hands up. 'That's all that I can ask. Another Blutop?'

Stanley held his mug forward and Plob topped him up.

'Look, Plob, I'm going to have a chat with my dad. But whatever happens there's no way that I'm going to pitch up with a thousand dragonriders or something. Firstly, you would be amazed at how few dragons there are in the known universe. Seriously - two ton, flying, fire-breathing mammals are not high on your average ladder of evolution. And secondly, if I can sway dad at all, it will be a gesture more than a solution. The pebble that starts the avalanche sort of thing.'

'As I said, mate. I'll take whatever I can get.'

'I think that I can get you four flyers that dad has a bit of a soft spot for. The best that you've ever seen.'

'Dragonriders?'

'Well, sort of. Spitfire pilots actually.'

'What's a Spitfire?'

'A sort of…mechanical dragon. Trust me, these boys know more about aerial combat than all of the Vagoths put together, but I can't promise anything.'

'Try, my friend,' said Plob.

'I will.'

And time and space curled up on itself and Stanley was gone.

'That,' said Spice. 'Is one seriously disturbing young man.'

'Right then. So, we will still be dead?'

Stanley nodded. 'Well, technically, yes.'

'So,' continued Smudger. 'Would we be like zombies? Don't know if I fancy that much, rotting to bits and walking around all stiff arms and legs.'

'No, no,' said Stanley. 'You see, you'll also,

technically, still be alive.'

'I don't get it. ' Smudger turned to the other pilots. 'Do you chaps get it at all?'

There was a chorus of no's.

'Look, it's simple. You're dead here. Do you accept that?'

The pilots nodded.

'Do you feel dead?'

Smudger shrugged. 'Not really, apart from the fact that I'm…well…here.'

'It's the same. You'll all be somewhere else but dead and still be like this.'

'Right,' said Smudger. 'So then, what's in it for us?'

'You get to fly again. And to fight.'

'You know, Stanley old chap, not to put to fine a point on it but I'll tell you something, flying and fighting again isn't something that fills any of us with a fervent desire. It's bloody terrifying; you spend half the time thinking you're about to die and the other half trying to make the other fellow die. It's no way to live, don't you know?'

'You'll get to fly dragons.'

Smudger smiled. 'Well, sure. I'll reserve judgement for that tall story.'

Stanley thought for a while. And then he said. 'You will be fighting for good against evil. You may be their only hope. They need you.'

Smudger sighed. 'Why didn't you just say so in the first place? I'm in. Gentlemen?'

'Yes.'

'Of course.'

'Lemon flavoured inner tube.'

Chapter 22

The dragon came streaking down out of the pale blue sky, pulled up at the last moment, fired three times at a tree near the end of the runway and then floated to a perfect landing. Plob dismounted, handed the reins to Boy and walked over to the group of Spitfire pilots.

Smudger, Jonno and Rufin were literally shaking with excitement, their eyes afire with a desperate need to fly one of these new, hereto mythical beasts. Belter, however, was looking decidedly ill.

'What do you think?' Asked Plob.

'Cracking,' answered Smudger. 'We all can't bloody wait.'

'Speak for yourself,' said Belter.

'Come on, Belter old chap,' said Smudger. 'Just like a ruddy great horse with fiery breath.'

'Yup. I hate horses. Reason I took up flying is to get as far away from bloody horses as possible. Can't trust any animal bigger than you are. And these buggers are the biggest I've ever seen. Ugly too.'

Boy, who had been listening, walked over, leading a dragon buy the reins. 'Here ye go, sir. You should be all reet wi' this one. It's called Buttercup. Very gentle.'

The dragon put its head down and looked closely at Belter. The spitfire pilot stood his ground but the blood drained from his face.

'Rub it ower the eye,' said Boy.

Belter raised a tentative hand and gingerly rubbed Buttercup on its eye-ridge. The dragon started to purr, a low rumbling sound like a thousand cats in a sound box.

'It's growling at me,' said Belter.

'Nay, sir. It's purring. She's happy.'

The dragon butted Belter, demanding more attention. The airman grinned and gave the huge beast a pat. 'Not so bad, are you?' He said. 'So,' he continued as he turned to Boy. 'Buttercup, hey?'

Boy shook his head. 'Nay, not really. I joost said tha' ta make you at ease. Her real name's Biter. But she'll nay bite yoo, she likes yoo.'

'How do you know?'

'Cause she ain't bit yoo yet.'

Boy gave the reins to Belter and then went back to the stables and led out a dragon for each pilot. Smudger got Inferno, Jonno got Blaze. Rufin got Flamer but he shook his head, pointed at his dragon and renamed it Pozar.

Plob and Spice gave the pilots a quick run down on how to control the dragons and they all mounted up.

'Follow me,' said Plob.

They thundered down the field in single file, wings beating the air as they all rose into the sky. Plob started with some straight and level flying to start, then a few gentle turns. He could see that the four airmen were totally at ease in the sky so he increased the difficulty factor some. High climbs, steep dives and sharp turns. After an hour or so he led them to the edge of the forest, picked a lone tree standing a little away from the rest, lined up, fired a shot at it and peeled away. Spice followed and then the four newcomers. Every single one hit.

Plob was well pleased and led the way home.

When they landed Boy was waiting for them, next to him, at shoulder height, captain Bhature hovered on his grav-cycle. Boy handed Plob a small sack. Plob looked inside to find a bunch of small, round bits of thin leather.

'Right, what are these?'

'Communicators,' said the captain. 'You slap the sticky side against the side of your neck and then you can speak to, and hear, anybody else who has one on.'

'Wow, awesome. Thanks.'

'I've issued some to master Smegly, the king and the T.A.D.S so that Biggest can keep better control of them. I've put the T.A.D.S on a different frequency to the flyers and I have allowed Smegly and the King a dual frequency option.'

Plob raised an eyebrow. 'Captain, I have no idea what you're talking about.'

'Sorry, you will be able to hear the flyers, Biggest will be able to hear the T.A.D.S and the master and the king can communicate with both.'

'Cool.'

Plob, Spice, the spitfire pilots and the rest of the dragonmen spent until late that day flying together. During this time Smudger used the communicators to drill the rules of aerial combat into them; keep the sun behind you, only fire at close range, attack from behind, if an opponent dives on you then fly up to meet him.

They mock battled over and over and over until the rules became rote with repetition.

That evening everyone went to bed early, tents pitched around the dragon stables. Ready. Waiting.

Chapter 23

Plob jerked awake to the sound of the bugle. Strident. Blaring. A call to arms. He dressed quickly and ran from the tent.

Boy was already up, holding Nim by his reins. Plob mounted, the first into the saddle. The rest of the flight was close behind him and they left the ground in a great gaggle. Plob slapped his communicator onto his neck and was immediately overwhelmed by chatter, at least six or seven voices talking at once.

'Hey,' he shouted. 'Shut it, all of you. No unnecessary chitchat. I talk, you answer unless it's needful. Do you all get that?'

There was a chorus of yes's and a single 'glue factory' from Rufin.

'Captain,' called Plob. 'Can you hear me?'

'Loud and clear, commander. Enemy approaching at approximately ten thousand feet, North West from your position.'

'Right, gentlemen, get some height and head for the sun. Let's see how high these beasts can go.'

The Dragonflight started to climb, vast wings beating gracefully against the rising sun, tall ships of the air. They rose quickly to around fifteen thousand feet where the air was thin and even the dragons were starting to labour to get enough oxygen into their huge lungs. They flew straight and level, the sun behind them, heading towards the enemy.

'Commander, RADAR shows that they should be visible soon.'

Plob strained his eyes and, sure enough, a gaggle of dots on the horizon, slowly getting bigger. It looked like thirty bandits, twenty fighters and ten heavies.

'Wingman Smudger,' said Plob.

'Commander?'

'Suggestions?'

'We dive at them out of the sun, punch through the formation to break it up and then turn hard and hit them from behind. Remember, only fire when you see the white of their dandruff.'

'Everyone ready?'

'Yes- wotcha - ready - placenta.' Came the replies.

'Let's go…whoopee.'

And like the wrath of gods the Dragonflight dove. When they were almost on top of the enemy Plob opened fire. Three quick rounds. All three hit the leading heavy.

Everyone else opened up at the same time, blasting over thirty rounds of burning plasma into the Vagoth formation. They were so close it was hard to miss and seven enemies went down almost immediately.

And then they were through and turning hard. A Vagoth fighter drifted in front of Plob and he squeezed off two rounds, hitting the dragon in the wing. It spiralled out of control. He felt a crackle of heat as a ball sizzled past him at close range.

'Behind you, Plob!' Shouted someone.

He turned hard and then jinked the other way, throwing off his attacker. To his left he saw Rufin flying his dragon perilously close to an enemy heavy and then firing at almost point blank range. The enemy literally exploded in front of him. Plob turned inside his attacker and burnt him from the sky.

A Vagoth had latched onto Spice and was following her through her evasive manoeuvres, twisting and turning with her. Plob dropped in behind him and blasted him out of the saddle.

'Thanks, oh mighty commander,' called Spice.

Plob latched onto a heavy and pumped four rounds into it, sending it screaming to the ground. He looked around him for another target but the air was empty.

He could see a number of smoking pyres in the distance but any other dragons were mere specks on the horizon as the aerial combat had scattered them far and wide.

'Spice?'

'Alive and well. Heading for home.'

'Smudger?'

'Present.'

'Rufin?'

'Melons.'

One by one the dragon flight checked in as they flew homeward. But Canjo, Baron Waldork's son, and Plage, the king's cousin, were not to be heard.

'Anyone see Canjo or Plage?' Asked Plob.

'Plage went down as we attacked,' answered Spice. 'Crashed into a Vagoth heavy. They both went down.'

'Canjo?'

No one answered.

That evening the Dragonflight celebrated. The defence had been a spectacular victory. For the loss of two men they had brought down twenty-two Vagoths, nine heavies and thirteen fighters.

But two families did not celebrate. Nor would they for a very long time. Fair mention would be made of the young heroes who died for their country, burials would be conducted with military honours and plaques would probably be set.

But none of those things will bring back a son, or friend or brother.

Typhon raged and ranted, erupted with exasperation, screamed and seethed and stormed and spluttered and shouted out his spleen as he strode about the room. 'What, in the name of all that is buggery bollocks, happened out there?'

Herr Gobling shrugged, a gesture that brought his multiple chins into blobby relief as the lapped against his jawbone. 'They were expecting us.'

'So? They were expecting us all of the times before. How did we suddenly become so useless?'

'I think, perhaps, my Fuhrer, they have gotten better. Their dragons have increased firepower, and they flew...like veterans. Something rather radical has happened.'

'It's your fault,' shrieked Typhon as he pointed at Gobling. 'You control the dragon corps. Their failure is your failure. You fat, baby-blue-clad, effete, loser.'

'Really, Herr Typhon, I must …'

Typhon held up his right hand, middle digit extended. The four-inch razor sharp talon on the end twinkled in the overhead light as he waved it back and forth. 'Would you like me to stick this in your eye?'

'Umm - No?'

'You're darn rooty-tooty right. So, shut the bollocks up and listen. If they can increase their firepower, so can we. Put some people onto preparing a new fire-feed for the beasts. Also, I want to see more flight training. Much, much more. Understood? As well as that, we need to start preparing for a huge breakthrough into their dimension so I want Goblin capture and storage increased ten times. I aim to send five hundred dragons over so I'm going to need a proverbial lavatory-full of those little green skinned creatures.'

Gobling nodded, saluted and left the room.

Chapter 24

Some people hug trees.

Other people hug rocks...this is because they don't have any trees.

But some other people, the ones that are called 'The Rockriders of Rohan', well...they do neither. What they do, in point of fact, is; they farm rocks.

And not just any old rock...oh no - the Rockriders of Rohan farm the semi-sapient rocks of the Rohan mountains. Rocks that start off as small boulders and grow, over time, into the mightiest rocks that ever trundled the paths of Rohan.

Fully trained Rohanian Rocks fetched a huge price on the open market and were used for any manual job that needed great strength. Pushing trees down, levelling ground for building on, rolling out roads and general demolition.

The Riders captured the rocks when they were still small foal-boulders and then kept them in fenced kraals, feeding them on a diet rich in quartz and granite until they were year old colt-rocks, large but clumsy, and, finally, fully grown Bulwarks.

It was at this stage that training started. Colts were introduced to the reins and the gimbal-saddle on which the rider sat. The gimbal-saddle was an ingenious combination of gimble-bearings and tracks that allowed the saddle to float freely on the top of the boulder no matter which way, or even how fast, it turned.

It needed immense skill to stay on the saddle of a fully-grown Bulwark as opposed to falling off and being crushed under twenty tons of rolling rock.

Master rockrider, Halcyon, stood on the edge of a cliff, looking over the Wibwok valley. Far below him the kraals of the Rohan were spread out. Round thatched huts and small fences. There was no point in putting up large fences as a full grown Bulwark could pretty much crush anything in its path. But the rocks were well trained and had been domesticated for many years so they stayed in their allotted boundaries.

High above him a flight of Vagoth dragons cut through the sky, Halcyon's Bulwark trundled slightly as it sensed the flying creatures. The rockrider patted his rock and gentled it with soothing words.

The Rohanians were a peace-loving nation, interested only in the herding of rocks, tie-dyeing of clothes and the smoking of various mountain herbs. But, try as they might, it was hard to love the Vagoths, a warlike peoples that revelled in all that was wrong. Halcyon shuddered as he watched the dragons. It was unnatural to be bound to the sky in such a way as opposed to being one with mother earth and her rocks.

He shook the reins and his Bulwark rolled forward, down the almost vertical cliff face as Halcyon perched expertly on his gimbal-saddle.

As he rumbled down the pathway to his kraal, his wife, Harmony, came out of the hut to greet him. 'Peace, husband mine.'

'And peace on you, chick. How are the sproglings?'

'They're cool, like, you know, Amity's catching

some Z's and Pacific is feeding the foal-boulders.'

Halcyon climbed down from his Bulwark. 'Harmony, we've got, like mondo problems. I mean, not us as a couple, we're copasetic, I mean like us as a people.'

'Why, what's up?'

'Well, I went to visit old Gumfroh, you know him, that gnarly old goblin dude that lives up in the Keldon grottos. I was like, keen to score some mushrooms from him and, like, when I got there….empty, man. Like someone ripped off all the goblins and split.'

'Wow,' said Harmony. 'That's, like…sad.'

'No, no…it gets worse. When I searched the caves for them I came across a couple…'

'Oh, that's good.'

'Negatory, babe, they were, like, deceased. Like, blood and gore and brain boogers all over the place. A real slash fest.'

'Major bummer, husbanamanund. So what do we do now?'

'No, wait…it gets worser. I, like, took a ride to the Prendon grottos and - same thing. Just a few dead little green dudes and the rest of the place full of emptiness. I'm, like, wigging out.'

'We need to tell the Honcho.'

Halcyon nodded. 'You're right, babe. The Honcho needs to know. This is, like… heavy.'

'I think that I can send some of us over to their side,' said master Smegly.

'Sounds good,' said king Bravad. 'How many?'

'Not sure. Probably only two. Maybe three.'

'Why so few?'

'Because I'm not prepared to use blood sacrifice and to gain enough power to shift more than that across the divide would need a lot of blood.'

'I think that I should go take a look then,' said Plob.

'Count me in,' added Smudger.

Smegly nodded. 'Right. When will you go?'

'Let's get it over with,' said Smudger. 'As me old mum always said, He who hesitates is lost so always look before you leap because fools rush in where angels fear to tread.'

'That doesn't make any sense,' said Plob.

'Cause not. She also used to say that, wise men think alike and fools never differ. She knew all of the old proverbs, did mum, she just never really got the hang of using them.'

Together with master Smegly they wandered down to the dragon pens, saddled up, took off and then circled the field, waiting as instructed.

'So how does this work?' Asked Smudger.

'Not that sure. I assume that the master is going to use a combination of professor Gombleberries internal advancer, doctor Dogrelpot's massive launcher and, most probably, a thunderbolt to provide the energy.'

'Will it hurt?'

'It'll be uncomfortable.'

'Oh, that's okay. Pain I'm not fond of, but discomfort I can live with.'

And the world around them went purple and sticky. And a huge thunderbolt smashed into them and blasted them from here to there whilst the two combined spells stopped their associated molecules from becoming disassociated.

It was like being rolled up in a carpet and then repeatedly kicked by a team of football hooligans while being force-fed a wet feather pillow covered in Tabasco.

'Golly,' said Smudger. 'This is uncomfortable.'

Another dragon exploded.

Typhon turned to Gobling and shook his head. 'Bang. Always they go bang. What are you doing with them?'

'My Fuhrer, we have increased the volume of brimstone to charcoal in an attempt to get more firepower from the beasts. It works, apart from the minor explosion glitch.'

'I see, and to a turkey, Christmas is a minor inconvenience.'

'I don't know what a turkey is, my leader. Or Christmas.'

'Whatever. Right, for a start - why do we put a flyer on the dragon every time that we test the new feed?'

'A dragon needs a flyer, sir.'

'I'm sure that they can explode quite well without one. Carry on experimenting, but do so without the flyer.'

'But, my leader…'

'Do as I say, or you go and sit on the next dragon.'

'I understand, great leader.'

And very, very high above, at the limit of the dragon ceiling, flew two non-Vagoth Dragonriders.

'Why are they blowing up their dragons?' Asked Smudger.

'Experimenting,' answered Plob.

'How do you know?'

'Trust me. Look, let's get out of here, head for that forest on the edge of the city, maybe hide the dragons and go in on foot, take a look around.'

'Righty-ho.'

They both stood up in their saddles and dropped straight down, flaring out at treetop level and gliding to ground in a clearing in the forest.

They led the dragons under cover and strapped a feedbag full of peat to their snouts before starting off towards the city that they had seen.

After a few yards Plob stopped. 'Wait, this is a pretty thick forest. I think that we should mark our trail so we can find our way back.'

'Good idea, what do you recommend? A trail of bread crumbs?'

Plob laughed. 'No, we'll simply cut marks in the trees.'

'No you won't.'

'Why not?' Asked Plob.

'Why not what?'

'Why can't we cut the trees?'

'You can if you want,' said Smudger.

'No you bloody well can't. Cut yourself instead, you knife wielding nutcase.'

Plob and Smudger stared at each other. Plob spoke first.

'Okay, who said that?'

'I did.'

'Well come out where we can see you.'

'You can see me.'

The two men stared into the forest.

'No, sorry. Can't.'

'I'm directly in front of you, you moron.'

Plob looked in front of him. Then he looked up. And down. 'The tree?'

'Yes the tree. The Oak tree that you wanted to cut because you were too lazy to simply ask for directions. I mean, really, how would you like it if I came to your house and started cutting up your friends just so that I knew where I was? Oh, look, the sitting room, slash, slash. Hmm, the kitchen, stab, cut. Bloody psychopath.'

'You can walk?' Asked Smudger.

'No, of course not. I'm a bloody Oak tree.'

'Well then how could you come around to my house?'

'Look, you, it's an example, obviously I won't actually come to your house, but you are, in actual fact, here and you were, in reality, about to cut me up for no good reason.'

'I'm really sorry,' said Plob. 'It's just that, where we come from trees aren't actually sentient beings. They don't talk.'

'Wow,' said the tree. 'So they're all dead?'

'No. Not dead. Sort of alive, I mean they grow and need water and stuff...'

'I see, but they don't talk so you amuse yourselves by cutting them up with your nasty sharp knives. Man, you guys are real psychos. Oh look, a mute, cut him up - ha ha ha. You make me sick.'

'Oh give it a rest, Oak.'

Plob and Smudger looked around, trying to see who else had just joined the strange conversation.

'Oh, excuse me, mister Beech, excuse me for talking, I'm sure.'

'They've apologised, they're obviously not from around here so why don't you just give it a break?'

'I'll give you a break, you snot nosed bogey.'

'Typical playground response. Grow up.'

The Oak tree shook furiously. 'You're lucky that I can't move or I'd come over there and smash you face.'

'Ha, please. I don't have a face.'

'Gentlemen...er...gentletrees,' said Plob. 'May you tell us the way to the city?'

'Sure,' said the Beech. 'Go past me, downhill, until you get to the steam. Then follow the steam and that'll take you there. Simple stuff. If you do get lost, ask any tree and they'll put you right.'

123

'Thank you,' said Plob as they walked away.

'Bah,' said the Oak. 'I hope that you get Beech bark disease.'

'Now that's just mean,' replied the Beech.

'Sorry…didn't mean that.'

'It's alright.'

'Thanks.'

The Honcho sat cross-legged next to the fire. He was dressed in a homespun tie-dyed tunic and shod with leather flip-flops. The only hint of his role of appointed leader was the simple wreath of daisies around his head.

'So, Halcyon, it seems like you're on a major bad trip, dude, like, what's wrong?'

'Well, Honcho, I was up at the grottos trying to score some mushrooms off the little green dudes and, like, they're all gone.'

'Wow, man…like, gone out of it or like, gone away?'

'Like vamoosed, chief. And then I found some that were there but they were, like, no longer with us on account of having had their heads bashed in. Then I went to the other grotto and it was, like, the same thing. It was, like, super-intense, you know.'

'Major downer, dude. Tell me, high priestess, what does the Goddess have to say?'

Wicconia, the high priestess of the Rohanians stood up, her grey hair tumbled to her waist and her web-thin tunic flowed about her as if driven by unseen winds. She raised her hands above her head and spoke. 'By Earth, by fire, by wind and sea and sky, I call on you, great Earth Mother. By the three hares of the Silk Road and the three moons of our faith I entreat thee. By Yin and by Yang and P'tangyangkipperbang…I beg your guidance.'

The fire flared high and a voice, as sweet as plum sugar and as soft as moonlight, soared around the camp.

'Death of a salesman. How green was my valley. Rock of ages. The avengers. People like us. Kill Bill. The flying Scotsman. War and Peace.'

Wicconia fell to her knees and wept.

The Honcho went over to her a comforted her. 'Like, hey, priestess dude. Chillax. No need to cry.'

'Oh there is, my Honcho, for we, the rockriders of the Rohan, have been called to war.'

'Like, wow. This I do not, you know, like at all. War is counterproductive. I mean, all this eye for an eye stuff, it's heavy to the max and eventually, like, it just leaves the world full of blind people. Anyhow, how do you know that we have to do war on someone?'

'The Earth Mother has spoken and I have seen the hidden words in her speech. Death, green, avengers, rock, people, kill, flying, peace. *Death* has befallen the *green* people and must be *avenged* by the *rock people* who must kill the *flying* people, or Vagoths, to bring *peace.*'

'Woah, this is, like, crap-o-mundo. Those Vagoth dudes are, like, super-paranoid war mongering buttheads. This me no like.'

'Like or not, Honcho,' said the High Priestess. 'This is your destiny. To lead the rockriders of Rohan to war.'

Chapter 25

Plob had to admit, the Vagoth city was very impressive. Buildings as high as five stories and constructed of grey stone towered above them. The roads were paved with tight fitting black cobbles and wherever you looked the Vagoth flag fluttered proudly, its red mailed fist on black background standing erect for all to see.

Smudger, however, had gone white with rage.

'What's wrong, Smudger?' Asked Plob.

'Goddamn Nazis.'

'What?'

These Vagoths, they're Nazis. The flags, the architecture the uniforms.'

'Settle, Smudger. We're here to recce, not to rush around killing random people.'

The pilot reined his emotions in and they continued their walk through the capital.

After three hours they had pinpointed what looked like the palace, the barracks and, on their way out of the city, the dragon pens. Neither of them said anything, but the size of the dragon pens was more than disturbing. It stretched for acres and acres. Hundreds and hundreds of pens as well as huts for workers, multiple feed stores and tackle rooms beyond imagining.

'How many do you reckon?' Asked Smudger.

'Not sure. Seven, maybe eight hundred. Maybe more.'

'I think more.'

'Good,' said Plob. 'Enough for all of us then.'

Smudger smiled and patted him on the back.

They meandered out of the city, walking slowly and aimlessly so as not to attract attention. After following the river for a while, looking for the tributary that their stream joined at, they eventually had to admit to each other that they were lost.

'Not a problem,' said Smudger. 'We simply walk into the forest, ask a tree and Robert's your mother's brother.'

'Okay,' said Plob. 'Let's go here.'

The two of them cut into the forest next to a tributary that may, or may not, have been the one that they had followed into the city. After they had gone a fair way into the forest they stopped.

'Hello, trees,' said Plob. There was no answer. 'Um…trees? Can you hear me?'

'We'd like some directions,' added Smudger. 'Could one of you please talk to us?'

'Don't be stupid, we're trees. Trees don't talk.'

'Well who said that?' Asked Plob.

The two dragon flyers waited while there was a chorus of whispering and a shaking of leaves.

'I'm a bush.'

'Don't be silly, we know that you trees can talk.'

More whispering.

'Not necessarily…maybe it's someone throwing their voice. Some sort of arboreal ventriloquism.'

'Well then, who's throwing their voice?' Asked Plob.

Whisper, whisper.

'You?'

'Oh come on, that's just stupid.'

'Yeah, well...how do we know that you're not a pair of woodcutters come to murder us unsuspecting evergreens?'

'We don't have axes.'

Whisper.

'Alright, where do you want to go?'

'Well,' said Plob. 'I'm not entirely sure. We followed a stream to get to the city. We got directions from a Beech. He said that if we get lost then all we needed to do was ask how to get back and a tree would tell us.'

'Well, yes, theoretically. But one would have to know where you wanted to end up or else one could simply be giving directions to a totally random place. Tell you what, give us a hint.'

'There was a really belligerent Oak tree there.'

'Hmm...sorry, doesn't help. All Oak trees are belligerent, most of them are so far up their own tap roots with their, "Ooh, look at me, I'm a deciduous broadleaf," looking down on us evergreens like we're the shirt tail relatives. Up theirs.'

Far away the flyers heard something shout, 'Up yours, needle leaf.'

'I don't mean to push,' said Plob. 'But can you help?'

'Yeah, sure. I'll just have to send out a few tweets, see what's going on, get some feedback and I'm sure that I can set you on the right path.'

'Tweets?' Asked Smudger.

'Yep, I'll use the twitter network. All of us trees do, well; we have to on account of not being able to walk. Hold on, here's a likely candidate,' said the tree as a sparrow landed on one of its branches. 'Hey, bird, do me a favour would you and see if you can find where these gentlemen came from.'

The bird cocked its head to one side and twittered

back.

The tree laughed. 'Yes, I know. You can find your way home from another continent and they get lost in a shrubbery. Still, they seem nice even though they are so directionally challenged, now go tweet tweet to all your friends and get back to me.'

The bird fluttered off and disappeared into the forest.

'Ok,' said the fir tree. 'The city, hey? What's it like?'

'Not bad,' said Plob. 'A lot of really big buildings.'

'Is that so? Wow.' The three stood for a while in silence (especially the tree who was a world-class stander). 'Right,' the fir continued. 'What's a building?'

The fortified garrison of Vogania squatted like a huge stone toad in between two grass-covered hills.

Although the garrison's walls were nowhere near as big as the main city of Lutetia, they were still twelve foot thick at the base and some six foot wide at the top. They stood over twenty feet high. Every twenty paces was a reinforced rampart behind which stood a group of bowmen. The gate was ironclad oak with a steel portcullis. There was no moat because there was no need for one.

The garrison had stood for over one hundred years. An unconquerable symbol of the might of the Vagoths. Unassailable, insurmountable, impregnable…and about to get its big stony ass kicked.

Four thousand rockriders of Rohan appeared on the skyline of the overlooking hills, their hair tied up in ponytails, recurved bows in their hands and quivers of arrows on their backs.

A mighty horn did sound and echo around the hills. And the war cry of the rockriders of Rohan was heard for the first time in over three hundred years.

'Riders,' shouted Halcyon. 'Let's Rock and Roll.'

The thunder of rolling Bulwarks was so loud that it seemed to be the very sound of the heartbeat of Mother Earth herself. The rockery swept down on the garrison and the riders started firing their bows as soon as they came in range.

The Vagoths fired back but it was hard to hit the fast moving riders as they thundered towards them.

'This is not a test,' shouted Halcyon.

'This is Rock and Roll.' Shouted the rest of the riders.

'We might be too old to Rock and Roll.'

'But we're too young to die.'

And the Bulwarks struck the wall like the second coming. Sheets of arrows swept riders from their rocks and Vagoths tumbled from the walls as the riders returned fire. The Bulwarks struck again and the huge wall crumbled. The rockriders rolled in, killing all before them.

Once the riders were inside the garrison the fight became a rout. A man in a black uniform with silver trim waved a white flag from a window in the central keep and Halcyon commanded his riders to stop.

'Come on out, dude. Let's, like, parley.'

The Vagoth officer walked out, flag held above his head. 'We surrender.'

'Good call, man,' said Halcyon. 'Excellent. Now, take your wounded and your non-wounded and, like, your cooks and stuff and go tell your Honcho that it's over. The reign of the Vagoth dudes is, like, over. Tell him that the rockriders of the Rohan are coming and that we're, like, seriously pissed.'

The officer nodded. 'May I ask why?'

'Sure, man, it's because you dudes need to learn that you can't sleep beneath the trees of wisdom, when your axes cut the roots that feed them. Now go, this is no longer your land.'

'There's a lot of them,' said Plob. 'I'd say seven or eight hundred. And that's just the ones that Smudger and I saw. There might be more.'

'This is a major problem,' said master Smegly. 'If Typhon manages to create enough power to send even half of those here at once then we are up the proverbial.'

'Got any suggestions, Plob?' Asked king Bravad.

'Smudger and I were talking…I think that we should break through again with two fighters and a heavy and try to destroy the palace. There's a good chance that Typhon will be there. We get him and our problems are over.'

'And if we miss him,' said the king. 'Then we kill a lot of innocents. Scullery maids, pages, cooks. I don't like it. Master Smegly, your thoughts?'

'Even if we kill him there is going to be considerable collateral damage. However, I don't see that we have a choice.'

'Who would go?' Asked Bravad.

'Myself,' said Plob. 'Belter and Rufin on the heavy.'

'But nobody understands Rufin,' said Braved.

'Doesn't matter. He understands us and whoever is flying the heavy is going to have to get low down and dirty, and Rufin has more bollocks that any other flyer I've ever seen.'

'I agree,' said Smudger. 'Enormous bollocks. Size of a pair of grapefruits.'

'Right,' said the king. 'Plob, make it happen and may the gods forgive us.'

Chapter 26

Science officer Roti rubbed his eyes with the heel of his hand. He was exhausted. He had spent the night working on a series of equations that were to the mind what an iron-man triathlon was to a body.

He was working on a hypothesis involving string theory, which is basically how gravity and quantum physics fit together. Using string theory he had come to the conclusion that the Paratha had not been sucked into a black hole but had, in fact, being subject to a wormhole in space.

Now, if one worked on the theory that wormholes are warps in the fabric of space-time that connect one place to another, and then one added the fact that black holes and wormholes are so similar at a quantum level that it is difficult to tell them apart then…then…something about a black hole compressing things, shrinking them down to a singularity.

Roti shook his head. He knew that he was on to something important but it kept sliding away from him like a bar of soap in the bath. He took a deep breath, stretched, and bent, once more, over his keyboard.

The three dragons flew in with the setting sun behind them. The fighters flew high and the heavy came in low, just above treetop level.

'That's the palace directly in front of you, Rufin. The one with white roofs and golden spires. Go in hard, Belter and I will keep any enemy fighters off your back. When you're out of fire, head for the forest rendezvous point and the master will bring you back. Got it?'

'Rotating wagon eel pie!' Shouted Rufin as he flew the two-headed monster close to the tallest spire and opened fire.

Huge balls of flame rolled out of the heavy's mouth and struck the base of the tower. The new improved feed meant that the fire didn't simply burn, it exploded in a shower of vicious white-hot plasma and the spire tumbled to the ground. Rufin kept the dragon low and pumped round after round into the palace, wreaking a terrible destruction.

'Bandits, five o'clock,' said Belter. 'Twenty plus taking off from the field. They're coming to join the dance.'

'Let's get them,' called Plob.

'Tally Ho!'

The two dragons plummeted down towards the Vagoths. Plob and Belter both waited until the last possible moment and then opened fire.

Plob took out two Vagoths with his first burst and Belter did the same. Then they were both turning and climbing and banking for their lives.

Plob kept a look out for Rufin because the moment that he had done his job and had gotten out of harm's way then Plob was out of there. He wheeled hard right and popped off a spray of rounds, more to confuse things than to actually hit someone as it was all about staying alive and keeping the Vagoth's attention off Rufin and on him and Belter.

Out the corner of his eye he saw Rufin powering towards the forest, still keeping low as he went.

'Another twenty seconds,' he informed Belter. 'Then we're gone.'

'With you, commander.'

At the exact count of twenty both of them broke off and drove their beasts hard and high, jinking from side to side to put off enemy fire. At the zenith of their climb, they turned and dove towards the rendezvous point above the forest. They arrived there seconds after Rufin on his slower heavy dragon and then, the universe folded around them and they were gone.

'Gooballs,' said Typhon. 'What is happening to my palace?'

'It appears to be burning, my Fuhrer.'

'Really, you think? Tell me, Gooballs, are you always an idiot or is it just when I'm around? Herr Gobling, how did this happen? Why weren't your vaunted dragon fighters in the air in time to stop this?'

'We were taken by surprise, my Fuhrer. Really, it wasn't my fault.'

'Well,' said Typhon. 'I could agree with you but then we'd both be wrong. Of course it's your fault.'

'But, my Fuhrer, I think…'

'Gobling, hush…listen carefully…do you hear that? That's the sound of no one caring what you think.'

Boredman giggled, a high-pitched adolescent titter.

'What's so funny, hamster eyebrows? Actually, Boredman, I've been meaning to have a chat to you for some time, now. What do you actually do? Seriously, what is your function in this ship of fools? I mean, you're about as useful as rubber lips on a woodpecker. Now, tell me, gentlemen, what the hell is going wrong here? Not only is my palace burning to the ground but, on top of this, I have heard that a bunch of hippies have managed to destroy the Vagonia garrison, and that was meant to be impregnable.'

'We were taken by surprise, my Fuhrer.' Said Gooballs.

'Oh, another surprise, my what an absolutely astounding day we're having with all these surprises. Tell me, my compact colleague, how does one get surprised by four thousand ravage-bent reprobates riding rocks to render ruin upon my redoubt?'

'They're a peaceful people, my leader. We never suspected they would attack us.'

'And why did they?'

'I think that they were pissed at us because we took their candyman away.'

'Candyman?'

'Drug suppliers, my Fuhrer. The goblins that supplied them their magic mushrooms, smoking herbs and suchwhat.'

'They would go to war over some dried mushrooms?'

'Well, they take their leisure time very seriously, my Fuhrer.'

'Whatever, take the army, find them and kill them. Then burn their villages to the ground, kill all of their livestock and…um…sow the ground with salt. Oh, yes, and write them out of the history books. That should take care of that little problem. Now please leave…I want to be alone.'

Chapter 27

Plob was white faced with anger and his entire body shook with pent up fury.

'Be careful, my boy,' said Bravad. 'I am not only your friend…I am your king.'

'I apologise, sire.'

'Plob, I understand how you feel, but the master and I made a decision; as soon as you came back we were to send a second attack. There's no way that they would expect it and we have told them to take out as many dragon pens as possible. Smudger had to go as he was the only flyer besides you that knew the layout. Jonno flew the heavy.'

'But why Spice?'

'Because she's one of the best flyers that we have. This is a war, Plob. More than a war, it is a frantic fight for survival. We have to make tactical decisions based on things other than who loves whom, or who wants who protected. Now go and rest, you've done well.'

Plob stalked from the room, his legs felt disjointed and weak from the after effects of his fear for Spice's safety.

'Dinna fash yourself, Plob,' said Boy. 'She's with two good men and she's no mean flyer herself. She'll be fine.'

As it happens, Boy was wrong.

The Vagoth flying scouts had seen the rockriders of the Rohan coming and so the occupants of garrison Bumsenfaust had prepared themselves for the attack.

Halcyon stood on top of his Bulwark and surveyed the scene before him.

'Hey, like, the soldiers dudes have dug trenches across the valley to, like, impede our progress. Also, they've set up a row of ballistae on the ridge there and I can see some, like, arrogantly large catapults in the actual garrison itself. All in all, you know, like, a good job.'

'So,' said the Honcho. 'What do you think that we should do?'

'Hey, Honcho, I don't know. I'm a lover, not a fighter. I mean, like, the extent of my military capabilities thus far is pretty much, like, charge and see what happens. This one calls for a little more sophistication.'

'It's worked so far.'

'Yeah, like, once. I think that what we need is a slight variation on the charge. Honcho, could you call all of the kraal leaders here, I think that I've got an idea.'

The Honcho sent two riders to fetch the kraal leaders and, within fifteen minutes, they were all crowded around Halcyon.

'Okay, dudes, I want you to round up all of the foal-boulders, colts and even wild-rocks that you can find. And I mean, like, all of them. Then we're going to drive them down the pass, in front of us. You reckon you can do it?'

There was a chorus of, 'right on,' and 'way to go,' and 'rock of ages, dude,' and the riders trundled off to do as bid.

Two hours later the garrison commander watched

Plob 3

in astonishment as his plate of food vibrated across the table and fell to the floor. And then pictures started to fall off the walls and furniture jiggled slowly sideways.

'Earthquake!' He shouted and ran for the door in order to get out of the barracks before they collapsed. As he got outside he was called by one of the sentries on the wall.

'Overcommander, up here.'

The Overcommander ran up the steps to the lookout. And saw the most amazingly terrifying thing that he had ever seen in his life. Thundering down the valley towards the garrison were thousands, no…hundreds of thousands of rocks, from small pebbles to massive, house size boulders. The very earth shook in sympathy and dust was thrown high and wide. When the rockery got to the trenches the boulders simply rolled in and filled them up. And behind them, shouting and hollering and hooting, came the rockriders of the Rohans.

The massive rockery hit the garrison walls with such power that it didn't even slow down, it simply flattened the entire fort. The riders swept in afterwards, firing their arrows into all that still moved. For they were the rockriders of the Rohans and they neither gave nor asked for quarter. Because…like a true nature's child, they were born to be wild.

Afterwards Halcyon and the Honcho sat atop their Bulwarks and surveyed the destruction.

'Hey, Honcho,'

'Yes, Halcyon my son?'

'Honcho, this is, like, bumming me out big time. I like this killing and destruction gig not at all. It's, you know, totally screwing with my karma. This is not how I saw my life going, a few days ago I was happy and at peace and now…'

'Ah, but Halcyon, Yesterday's just a memory, and tomorrow is never what it's supposed to be.'

'I just want to be free again, Honcho.'

The Honcho leaned over and grasped the rider by the arm. 'No one is free, Halcyon. Even the birds are chained to the sky.'

'Cool, dude. Cool.'

The three dragons materialised above the forest. Smudger took a few seconds to get his bearings and then he led them towards the barracks.

They kept as low as possible to avoid direction and, within minutes they were over the main dragon pens. They all opened up at the same time, flaming balls of plasma exploding in and around the pens. Spice closed her ears to the sounds of the dragons screaming and agony as they burnt and exploded.

Ten, twenty, thirty pens went up in smoke. The trio turned and burned again, fires marching down the rows of pens like a holocaust of retribution. Spice saw riders running from burning buildings, trying to mount their beasts. She fixed on them and blasted them to death.

'Bandits, twelve o'clock,' said Smudger. 'Lots of them, looks like we've been ambushed.'

'Jonno,' said Spice. 'Break off and head for the forest extraction point. Go! Smudger, let's see if we can slow these bandits down, give Jonno a chance to get his heavy away.'

The two fighters climbed to intercept the incoming Vagoths while Jonno urged his slow double-headed dragon back to the departure point.

Spice guessed about twenty Vagoths were diving down at them. She held her fire for as long as she could and, as she fired the Vagoths opened up. The air around her turned to fire. She felt her hair frizzling up and her eyebrows scorching off with a small puff. Her left sleeve caught alight and she beat at it frantically. Tempest screamed as a ball of plasma clipped her wing and she went into an uncontrolled spin. 'Pull out,' shouted Smudger.

At the last possible moment Tempest recovered and Spice drove her hard towards the forest. Smudger sprayed off as many rounds as he could before his dragon ran dry and then he flew after her.

But he could see that she was never going to make it. 'Take her down into the first clearing that you see, dismount and run like hell before they strafe you. Don't worry, Spice, I won't leave you.'

In the distance Spice saw Jonno reach the extraction point and wink out of existence as he went over to the other side. Tempest was labouring badly now, every flap of her giant wings a terrible effort. Spice saw a clearing and guided the dragon towards it. They half landed, half crashed into the ground. Tempest gave a final bellow and then lay still. Spice climbed down and ran under the trees for cover.

Smudger flared his dragon to a landing in the clearing, jumped down and smacked its rump. 'Go!' He shouted. The beast rose clumsily into the air and headed automatically to the extraction point, winking out as it got there.

Smudger ran into the trees to join Spice. 'Are you all right?'

'A bit burnt. Sod it, that was close. Mind you, not sure what we're going to do now.'

'I think that we should head towards the extraction point and then wait and hope for rescue. The only problem is, I have no idea where the extraction point is.'

'Well, you could always ask us for directions,'

said a voice.

'Is that a tree talking?' Asked Smudger.

'Don't be silly. Trees don't talk,' retorted the voice.

'They bloody well do.'

'Um, Smudger,' said Spice. 'I don't think that they actually do talk.'

'They do here. Plob and I had a long chat with them. They were very helpful.'

'Well they're not talking to you now,' said the voice.

'Well who is then?'

'Me,' said a small green skinned creature stepping out from behind a bush. 'Farticus, son of Flatuliticus, son of Bottomburpus at your service. I am a forest goblin from the noble line of the Intestinus family.'

'Pleased to meet you, Farticus,' said Smudger. 'I am Smudger, son of Terry, son of Charles. I am from the decidedly middle class line of the Smith family.'

'I'm Spice. I don't know my parents and my grandparents are dead.'

'Well, follow me, son of the middle class and daughter of the dead.'

'What about the Vagoths?' Asked Smudger. 'Won't they be trying to find us?'

'They will fly over the forest, but they will not enter. And if they do then they will not leave. The forest dwellers do not take kindly to the despoilers.'

They followed the goblin deeper into the forest and, as they walked, the light grew dimmer while night approached.

'We will need help to find accurate directions to whence you wish to go,' said the Goblin. 'It is difficult in the extreme to pinpoint an area of this so very large forest merely from instructions as vague as…somewhere over there. When we get to the village there are others who can help.'

'How large is your village, Farticus?' Asked Spice.

'Oh, large. Large enough.'

Almost without warning the three walkers came to a clearing. The open space measured perhaps two hundred yards across and above it, over one hundred giant trees had been bent towards the centre and lashed together to form a natural roof of leaves and branches. The clearing itself was lit with countless flaming torches and stalls and chairs and tables were strewn without pattern around the space. Some of the stalls were serving hot food, others served ale and spirits. A group of musicians strolled around playing their lutes and mandolins and hand drums, the tune slightly discordant but jolly nevertheless. The bulk of the beings were goblins but there were also a variety of bipedal and quadrupedal revellers in various shades of skin and fur colour.

'Welcome to the village of Fabianus, we are a collective group of like-minded beings living together in harmony. We have no leader, no social hierarchy and we are all equal. Come, before I introduce you around let us to my dwelling where you can refresh yourselves.'

The two flyers followed Farticus through the clearing and beyond, to a wide wooden staircase that was so steep as to almost be a ladder. They climbed while holding on to a rope banister to steady themselves.

Eventually they came to a landing near the top of the massive trees. From this landing spread a series of small walkways. Farticus led them along one of the walkways to a magnificent tree house. It was constructed from latticework reeds and bleached hardwoods so that it was light yet strong. The door opened into a general living area that sported a roof that could be opened via a pulley system. Large arched windows looked out across the treetops and a fire burned, small but bright, in a metal bowl in the centre of the room. At the far side of the room were three doors. Farticus showed them to the one and opened it. There was a small room with two feather mattresses on the floor and a pile of furs.

'The two of you can sleep here. Now, I am sure that the lady will want to use the room next door.'

He showed Spice to the next room. In it was a copper bath. Farticus pulled a lever and water ran from a tank in the roof, through a hollow bamboo tube and into the bath.

'You will find the water is pleasantly warm from the days sun, my lady. On the table there are various perfumes and unguents that you are free to use. Middle class Smudger and I will wait in the living room while you ablute.'

As soon as the men left the room Spice stripped down and sank into the bath with a sigh.

A while later the flyers and their new friend walked back down the stair ladder. This time Smudger noticed many more dwellings. He also noticed that the closer they got to the ground the less salubrious the dwellings became until, at almost ground level, they were little more than thatched platforms.

'Farticus,' said Smudger. 'Why are the living quarters down here so beastly compared to the ones at the top?'

'Oh, this is the prostratus level. I live in the dominatus level. In between we have both the upper and lower mesialus levels.'

'But you said that everyone was equal.'

'They are.'

'I beg to differ, mine host. Some of these dwellings are little more than a few mean planks strung together with hope and sisal.'

'Yes, and everyone on this level is equal to everybody else on this level.'

'And the level above?'

'The same.'

'No,' said Smudger. 'Is this level in any way equal to the level above?'

Farticus laughed. 'Of course not. That would be silly. And before you get too het up, middle class Smudger, I must tell you that all is decided on by voting and everybody gets a vote.'

'Well that seems fair.'

'Of course it is. As a member of the dominatus level I control ten votes. The middles control either three or four and the prostrarus levels get one vote per being.'

Spice touched Smudger on the arm and shook her head. 'We are guests,' she whispered to him.

Smudger nodded and stopped his line of questioning and they followed the forest goblin to the clearing where they were introduced all round.

Chapter 28

Halcyon stood in the mouth of the cave and stared out at the world beyond. In the distance he saw the Vagoth dragon scouts flying low. Searching.

Since the riders last great victory at Bumsenfaust they had been running, trying to escape the Vagoth dragons. And it was proving to be very difficult. They had sent all of the women and children to caves deep in the mountains and then the rockery had gone on the move. Travelling at night and hiding in caves during the day.

They had lost more than a dozen riders to dragon flame and many more had been injured. But neither Halcyon nor the Honcho had any idea how they were to combat the Vagoth air superiority.

The Honcho walked over and put his hand on Halcyon's shoulder.

'Mega bummer to the max,' he said.

'Extreme bummer,' agreed Halcyon.

'But we must always remember, my son, to gain that which is worth having we must be prepared to lose everything else.'

'Yeah, that's, like, a very hip groove, Honcho, but sometimes the losing hurts, man.'

'I dig what you're saying, Halcyon, but we have to be strong, the strongest blades are forged in the furnace of despair. We shall overcome because we are righteous dudes and none shall gainsay us.'

'Right on, brother. Right on.'

Plob winked into being above the forest. He took a few seconds to get his bearings. Coincidently this was exactly the same amount of time it took the wing of six Vagoth fighters to spot him.

Plob was flying a heavy as he needed a dragon that could carry three people and he had not let himself even contemplate that he may not find the other two alive. The Vagoths had every advantage; faster beasts, height and manoeuvrability. Plob turned to face them, swinging his beast's heads from side to side and pumping out rounds as fast as the heavy could, spreading a wall of fire across the sky. Two of the Vagoths plummeted, burning, from the air, but the Heavy was out of fire.

The young magician pulled hard left and drove his dragon down as low as possible jinking left and right in an attempt to throw the fighters off. But all he was really doing was buying a little time. Nothing more.

The first ball hit his dragon on the tail causing it to screech in agony. The next two took out its left wing and they tumbled out of the sky, smashing into the trees of the forest.

As soon as they hit the ground Plob jumped from the dragon and ran, narrowly avoiding the strafing run from the Vagoths who poured fire down at him. Trees on each side of him caught alight and the heavy dragon exploded as three rounds hit him.

Then there was a sound like an enormous sneeze and a vast geyser of muddy water leapt into the sky knocking two Vagoths off their mounts and sending them to an abrupt and messy death. The last two Vagoths peeled off and bugged out. Plob fell to the sod and gasped for air as the geyser of water fell back to earth and extinguished the fires.

'Are you all right?' Asked a voice.

'Hello,' said Plob. 'Is that a tree?'

'Don't be silly. Trees don't talk.'

Plob, who had absolutely no intention of becoming part of a running gag, said nothing.

'Why were the despoilers trying to kill you?' Asked the voice.

'Specifically because I'm at war with them,' said Plob. 'But generally speaking, I'm not sure. They simply pitched up one day and started burning the poo out of us.'

'Ah, that sounds like them all right. People call me Terrane, I am the lord of the loam. Whom might you be?'

'I might be Plob. Are you an invisible being?'

'Why would you say that?'

'Because I can't see you.'

'Yes you can.'

Plob scanned around, eyes searching the shadows. 'No, sorry.'

'Hold on, mayhap this will help.' The ground in front of Plob started to bulge, the grass peeled back and water flowed up from the earth. Plob stepped back in shock as the soil reared up and formed the shape of a man made from mud. 'Is this better?'

'You look like me.'

'Yes, I have modelled myself on you so as not to cause alarm.'

'Well it's a bit freaky, I can tell you that.'

The loam lord frowned. 'I'm sorry but I do not understand the concept – "Freaky".'

'You know, weird, strange.'

'Ah, unusual, unsettling. Here, let me…' the mud mans face shimmered and changed. Now he looked more generic. A face that was neither attractive nor unattractive. A completely unnoticeable face. Perfect for a spy, or perhaps a serial killer. Except, of course, for the undeniable fact that it was composed of mud.

'Thank you,' said Plob. 'That is better.'

'So, young human, how can I be of assistance to an enemy of the Vagoths?'

'I'm actually in a bit of a pickle, to put it mildly. What you have just witnessed is the very short and unsuccessful attempt to rescue two of my fellow flyers that were burnt down yesterday. Talk about a cock up, I don't have a dragon anymore, I don't know where I am and, if truth be told, I'm not even sure if my friends made it or not. In fact I didn't actually have much of a plan, I simply reckoned that if they had made it then they would hopefully try to get to our extraction point. So, there you have it.'

'Very succinctly put, young sir. If you could just wait a while I shall find out if your friends have entered the forest.'

The loam lord deconstructed and became a mere muddy plashe on the turf. Plob sat down on a boulder and waited. After about five minutes the pool of mud reconstructed and once again became a facsimile of a human.

'Your friends are here. They arrived last night and are currently the guests of the forest goblins.'

Plob punched the air with relief. Spice was safe. 'My lord, I thank you, that is very good news. Pray tell, how did you find out?'

'I merely communed with the forest floor. The earth and I are one and what it knows so do I, within the limits of this forest. Now, come with me, I shall guide you.'

The lord started to move and Plob followed. Watching the loam lord walk was decidedly disconcerting in that he did not take actual steps. Instead he morphed from one position to the next so that his feet never actually lost contact with the ground. A life sized claymation figure.

They had been walking in silence for a little over an hour when the loam lord stopped in a small clearing. He held up a hand to halt Plob. 'Don't move,' he whispered. 'Be still. Be quiet.'

The two stood for a while and then the lord dropped his hand. 'No, I was mistaken, it's not them.'

'Not who?' Asked Plob.

'The Arguementors. A feral group of rogue philosophers. They're extremely dangerous.'

'Why?'

'They drag you into a deeply unsolvable argument and don't let you go until you have answered the question to their satisfaction. Most of their victims die of thirst or exposure long before the termination of the argument. Of course they cannot harm me but you would be in terrible danger. Oops.'

'What do you mean, oops?'

'I made a mistake,' said the loam lord as he disintegrated back into a pool of mud.

Before Plob could register his surprise the forest all around him was filled with the sound of voices. It sounded like some sort of insane question and answer routine, a single voice shouting out a question and then a multitude of voices murmuring back the answer in unison.

'Question - Why did the chicken cross the road?' Asked the leading voice.

'Answer - The confluence of events in the cultural gestalt necessitated that individual chickens cross roads at this historical juncture, and therefore synchronicity brought such occurrences into being,' Mumbled the others.

'Question - What is the sound of one hand clapping?'

'Answer - Cl…'

'Oho, what have we here?' Said the leader as he walked into the small clearing and saw Plob.

'Umm…we don't know that one.' Said someone.

'I wasn't asking you. I didn't say, question, did I? No, so obviously it was a rhetorical question about something that I have just seen.'

'Well how are we supposed to know if we haven't seen what you've just seen? That would make it an aporetic question to us because how could we possibly answer it? It's an insoluble contradiction or paradox, I mean, "what have we here," could be referring to anything, anywhere.'

'Well come and have a look then.'

The rest of the philosophers wandered into the clearing. There were about twenty of them, bearded and unkempt, dressed in long grubby robes and carrying a variety of weapons.

'It's a man,' said the someone.

'Ah, but is it?' Asked the leader. 'Or is it merely a mass hallucination brought on by the inability to answer an aporetic paradox?'

Plob had decided that he had had enough.' Gentlemen,' he said. 'I think…'

'Aha!' Shouted the leader and the other one in unison. 'He exists. *Cogito Ergo Sum*. He thinks…therefore he is.'

The leader stepped forward. 'Welcome, young man who definitely exists. I am Plako, the philosopher. Perhaps you have come across my thesis, "I am real but is cheese also a god"?'

Plob shook his head. 'No sorry.'

'Really? It's quite famous, you know.'

'Well, I'm not actually from around here.'

'Ah, that would explain it.'

'Yeah, that and the fact that it's crap,' said one of the other argumentors.

'Who said that?' Shouted Plako. 'Come on, own up you crowd of insipid, pedantic, leather-tongued oracles of bourgeois intelligence. I bet it was you, Desmarties. How dare you, considering your doctorial farce; "If blind people wear dark glasses, why don't deaf people wear earmuffs?".'

'Your bum, Plako.'

Plob smiled to himself. He had no idea why the loam lord had called this bunch of eccentric middle-aged men dangerous. High spirited maybe. Argumentative, definitely…but dangerous?

'What do mean, my bum?' Asked Plako. 'You go to far, Desmarties.'

'No, sir. I do not go far enough.'

Plako pulled a throwing knife from his belt and whipped it overhand at the arguing argumentor. The blade struck him in the chest with a sickening crunch and he fell to his knees.

'The hour of my departure has arrived and we go our ways; I to die, and you to live. Which is better? Only God knows.' Said Desmarties as he fell to the ground.

The rest of the argumentors started clapping and hooting.

'Fantastic last words, old man.'

'Well said.'

Plako wiped a tear from his eye. 'What a great man he was. Brilliant last words. I hope that I can go as well as him.'

Plob's knees felt weak. Violent death was nothing new to him, but such casual brutal behaviour over mere semantics was new.

Plako walked over to the corpse and tugged the

dagger from his chest. It made a sucking sound that made Plob's wobbly knees pass their feelings of unsteadiness onto his stomach.

'Now, young man who definitely exists,' said Plako. 'It is time for us all to discuss some philosophy. Tell…if the universe ceased to exist - would the rules of chess still apply?'

Plob said nothing for a while. This was no mere argument…this was cutting edge debating - literally. One mistake and blood would flow. The first thing that the young magician did was relax and then attempt to draw magical power from his surrounds. But it was to no avail. This world had a different magical resonance to his home and was thus unusable by him.

So instead, he thought.

'Right,' he said. 'Okay, let us assume a few basic rules that we all might agree on. I am confident in the assumption; that which is, is. And that which is not, is not. Therefore, that which is not, cannot be is, because it is not. Do we agree?'

There was a general mumble of agreement amongst the argumentors.

'Yes, yes,' said Plakus. 'It's a basic form of Parmezaneez principle of what is and is not. Carry on.'

'Right - So assume that what the opposite of what I want to say is true, say that the universe stopped existing as you said, is would therefore be is not. Is not cannot be is. That's a contradiction and therefore cannot exist. As a result, and this is actually blindingly simple, the only possible answer to your question is…a fish.'

There was complete silence for at least a full minute and then one of the argumentors started to clap. Slowly the others joined in.

Plob grinned. 'So, can I go?'

'Oh no, absolutely not,' said Plako.

'But everybody's clapping.'

'Yes, they are. But not on account of you being anywhere near correct. They're clapping because you delivered your theory with such confidence. Panache is highly respected in the philosophical circles. However, your theory is a pile of poo.' So, sword or axe?'

'Sword or axe what?'

'Unfortunately, the punishment for producing such a faecal theory is fatal.'

'Sod that!'

'Look, young man who definitely exists, you seem like a nice person and so on and so forth but rules is rules.'

Plob's heart started to hammer in his chest so hard that his whole body seemed to bounce up and down in sympathy. Then he noticed that Plako was also bouncing slightly up and down at the same time. Even the trees were jiggling to the self same rhythm.

The ground next to Plob reared up to become the loam lord. 'I'd lie down if I were you,' he said.

Plob needed no further instruction and fell to the floor.

Trees were bent aside and a roaring, liken unto the sound of a tsunami smashing into Japanese whaling ship, reverberated across the forest. A hand the size of wagon descended, grasped Plakus and picked him up.

'Any last words?' Rumbled the owner of the vast hand.

'Man will never be free until the last ruler is strangled with the entrails of the last priest.'

A few of the argumentors who were running away paused briefly to clap.

'Good one, Plakus.'

'Way to go, ex-philosopher.'

A massive hand squeezed. Plakus squealed briefly and then went limp and was dropped to the ground. Plob looked up at his saviour. Two legs the size of oak trees. A barrel of a body and two arms that were far too long to be in proportion. Atop the whole massive assembly was to be found a head of gigantic proportions and, in the centre of the forehead, one round eye.

The massive being knelt down next to Plob and extended a finger for the young magician to shake. Plob did so.

'Greetings young enemy of the despoilers. My name is Robert, I'm an Ogre and I shall be your rescuer today.'

'Hi, Robert. I'm Plob. I shall be your rescuee. Many thanks. And thanks to you, my loam lord. I must admit, I thought that you had abandoned me.'

'Of course not, I merely went to get help. Now let us proceed to the goblin village.'

Plob shook fingers with Robert again and the ogre stomped off into the distance. Plob and Terrane continued on their way.

Chapter 29

Science officer Roti swung the accelerator gun over the table and pointed it at the sliver of fingernail that lay on the titanium protection plate. There was nothing unusual about the piece of fingernail. Mister Roti had clipped it off his left hand thumb earlier that day. He had spent the rest of the day with chief engineer Subji connecting the six weft motors in series as opposed to parallel in order to increase the power output to the woof drive by a factor of five.

'Right, captain,' said the science officer. 'As you know, the way that we travel through space is via the expansion of the empty space behind the craft thereby creating a perceived forward movement that is faster than light even though we are unable to perceive the movement due to the fact that we have not actually moved in space at all.'

'Roti, remember…five years learning to fly this massive piece of hardware. I know how to make it go but I have no actual idea why it does. That's your job.'

'Okay, I'm just laying the basics out here to avoid any misunderstandings. So, in order to achieve this we need to have access to horrific amounts of energy - basically equal to the mass-energy of a medium sized planet. Obviously we cannot carry a planet with us so what we did is create a tiny singularity or black hole that we keep in the woof drive.'

'I'm getting bored, Roti.'

'Hold on, captain, almost there. When we were caught in the random black hole that brought us here I think that it somehow reversed the polarity of the singularity in our woof drive.'

'So?'

'Watch,' said Roti. And he flicked a switch that powered up the accelerator gun.

The fingernail shimmered and then…grew. It grew until it was at least ten times its original size and then stopped.

'What just happened?' Asked the captain.

'What you have just seen, captain, is irrefutable proof that the people of this planet are not giants. They are the same size as us, however, we have been shrunk by the reversed polarity caused by our excursion through the black hole.'

Captain Bhature stood up out of his seat. 'By all the gods, Roti. Does this mean that you can make us normal sized again?'

'Theoretically, sir. But it took all of the power that we have to revert a small sliver of fingernail. I have no idea how we can raise enough power to revert the entire ship.'

'Well work on it, my friend. Work on it.'

'Aye aye, captain.'

Spice pulled Plob hard up against her and squeezed. 'You came.'

'Of course,' said Plob.

Smudger held out his hand and Plob took it. 'Well done for finding us, commander.' Said the fighter pilot. 'Did you bring a dragon?'

'Actual, Smudger, I've made a bit of a cock up of

the whole rescue mission thing. I brought a dragon but it's more than a little dead. Bits and pieces all over the forest actually. Bastards jumped me as I got here. Sorry about that.'

'Not a problem. I'm sure that we can make some sort of plan,' said Spice as she snuggled up against Plob and purred like a cat.

At the edge of the village clearing Farticus and a number of other dominatus level goblins were talking to lord Terrane. Plob noticed that the goblins were treating the loam lord with a respect that seemed to border on actual worship.

Terrane saw Plob looking at him. The loam lord raised his hand, waved, and then abruptly disintegrated. Gone.

The group of dominatus level goblins walked over to Plob, their faces serious.

'Greetings commander Plob, I am Farticus.'

'Greeting, Farticus,' said Plob with a commendably straight face.

'We have spake with the loam lord and he has commanded us. He has tasked us to stop hiding in the forests and to take fight to the despoilers. And, as he is our lord, we must obey, even though the mere thought of leaving the forest causes us great fear and sadness.'

'Wow,' said Plob. 'So Terrane is a big deal around here? I thought that you guys were more into trees.'

'Terrane is the loam. Without loam there are no trees. Without trees - no forest. He is our lord and saviour. So - we shall fight.'

'Works for me,' said Plob. 'The more enemies that the Vagoths have, the better for us. Is there any way that we can help?'

'On the contrary, commander, we must help you. How do you propose to get back to your kingdom?'

'At the moment, not that sure, to be honest.'

'The loam lord suggested that you steal some dragons from the Vagoths. Would you be able to fly them?'

'Sure. But how do we get them?'

'We will supply you with a guide. As well as this we plan to create a diversion whilst you are sneaking in. We are sure that it can be done successfully.'

'Sounds good. When?'

'Rest tonight, we plan to attack at first light. Commander, you can sleep in my abode with your lady. Middle class Smudger will be given an alternative place to slumber. Now, people, let us to bed.'

Chapter 30

Belief creates things.

Real things.

Father Christmas exists, ask any six year old. So does the Easter Bunny. And the bogeyman and the snakes that live under the bed. When we were young we could see their footsteps, they ate our mince pies and we heard them snuffling around the room when we had our head under the blanket.

Then we grew older we no longer believed. There are no longer any footprints, we buy our chocolate eggs from a supermarket and we sleep with the lights off.

Lack of belief can destroy things. No more Father Christmas. No more Easter bunny. No more Bogeyman. But they are never truly gone. They are still there, in the very back of our minds. Waiting.

And in the dark recesses of the minds of the cave-dwelling goblins lurked some very ancient beliefs that were being brought to the fore by Typhon's mass-sacrificing program. These were, the beliefs in the old ones. Those primeval beings that came before the gods. Those who were always there. The holy goblin trio.

Nyx; the god of night.

Nerus; the god of light.

Norgam; the god of all the other bits, including social faux pas, bodily functions, words that rhyme with orange, the infinite universe and fresh milk for the tea.

And so did the belief build up and the sun did set and the eldritch wind of creation did blow through the forest, feeding on newfound faith.

'Brrr,' said the Oak tree. 'Didn't fancy that wind much. Did you feel that?'

'Yep,' answered the evergreen. 'Felt eldritch it did.'

'Exactly what I thought,' said the Oak. 'Arthur, I said, that feels decidedly eldritch that does.'

'Who's Arthur?'

'Me,' answered the Oak. 'I'm Arthur.'

'Since when?'

'Since yesterday, if you must know. I'm sick of just being, Oak. You know how confusing it gets? There must be over twenty thousand of us in this forest alone. All answering to the same name. So, I says to myself, why don't you give yourself a name I says. So, Arthur it is.'

'Arthur's a silly name for a tree.'

'Well, excuse me. What would you use?'

'I don't know. Woody. Planky. Mister Timber.' The wind blew again. 'Ooh, Arthur, I'm scared.'

'Don't be evergreen, it's just a wind.'

'Arthur?'

'Yes.'

'Hold me.'

In the background a small Spruce sniggered.

Farticus woke the three flyers well before dawn, handing them each a cup of steaming chestnut coffee, a liquid as bitter as a critics ravings and a strong as over-ripe Stilton.

160

The clearing was full of goblins, all dressed in similar combinations of leather armour with jerkins of fish-scale steel mail. Instead of swords they favoured large curved daggers. There were some archers but the main carried either slings or three-foot long blowpipes that discharged poisoned darts.

Farticus unrolled a parchment and laid it on the ground. He used his dagger to point.

'Here are the dragon pens, on the West side. As you can see, there is a large barracks building on the East side. We aim to attack the barracks, thereby distracting the flyers from your endeavours. We will set fire to the buildings and then retreat back into the forest. Quick in, quick out. You will need to approach from the West, so will travel a separate route from the rest of us. To ensure that you don't get lost I have organised you a guide.'

A young goblin stepped forward. Unlike the others he was dressed in a plain brown jerkin with brown leather trews. He wore a wide baldric over his left shoulder and in it were slotted a selection of throwing knives.

'Hello, my name is Eeeek!'

'I'm sorry,' said Smudger. 'Eeeeeek?'

The goblin gave Smudger an odd look. 'No, Eeeek! Eeeeeek is the feminine version. If I had a sister she might be called Eeeeeek! I am simply Eeeek!'

'Sorry, old chap,' apologised Smudger. 'Do you mind if we just shorten it to Eek? Much simpler.'

'Actually I do mind. Eek is simply the onomatopoeic version of a scream. It's like calling someone Argh or Ouch. Bloody silly.'

'Right Eeeek!' Said Plob. 'Now that's all sorted, I am commander Plob, this is Spice, the slightly confused gentleman is Smudger. Pleased to meet you, what's our next step?'

'Simple. We go to the base, wait for the attack, sneak in, steal dragons, you go, I go, happy days.'

Lead the way,' said Plob.

Count Wolfgang Peesundbakon downed the glass of schnapps and poured himself another. 'My dear Pieter Spittleundflem,' he said. 'I would never say anything against the Fuhrer, all that I am saying is, we are fighting a war on two fronts.'

'Pah, hardly. A bunch of rock-riding hippies and a gaggle of amateur dragon flyers. I'd say one-and-a-half fronts at most.'

'Well, those one-and-a-half fronts have razed two of our garrison fortresses to the ground, levelled the palace and killed over twenty of our dragons in their pens.'

'But now, my count? The hippies are hiding in the hills and we shot down the last batch of amateurs that dared to violate our air space. As soon as the army can collect enough goblins together for the mass-sacrifice then we shall pour through the divide and overwhelm our enemies. After that, we come back here and burn the hippies to hell and back. End of story.'

'Still…'

The door to the mess burst open and Hienz Beenz ran in. 'Kaptein Peesundbakon!'

'What is it, Heinz?'

'We're under attack, sir.'

'Rockriders?'

'No, my kaptein. Goblins.'

Count Peesundbakon jumped to his feet. 'Arm yourselves people, quickly, to the walls.'

The flyers left the mess at a run, booted feet crashing in the wooden floors. As soon as they got outside they could hear the sounds of men screaming and dying. Sheets of arrows and a hailstorm of stones poured over the walls with dreadful accuracy.

'To the walls. Return fire. Sound the bugle.'

The young bugler started to blow, the call to arms rang, loud and urgent, across the encampment. Hundreds of flyers and soldiers ran to the walls and started firing back with bow and crossbows.

A small flask of lamp oil with a burning rag stuffed into the neck sailed over the wall and burst against the barracks. Immediately another twenty or thirty followed. The fire spread quickly, flames dancing high into the still morning air.

Eeeek! Held his hand up and the three flyers came to a halt. The goblin pointed.

'The fires have started. We must move quickly now.'

They all broke into a fast trot.

Private Albret Pawksosaje and private Gurted Schmaltzunpikel were watching the fight from the relative safety of the dragon pens. Both were eating sandwiches the size of a shoebox.

'Ooh,' said Albret, through a mouthful of sauerkraut and pigs knuckles. 'What's that?' He pointed at a new explosion that lit up the sky with flames of blue and green.

'Must be the schnapps stores,' answered Gurted. 'That'll teach the officers for storing all their booze instead of drinking it like normal people do.'

'Yeah,' agreed Albret. 'What's the point of having twenty year old schnapps when the stuff we brew ourselves fresh out of the still works just as well.'

'If it doesn't make you go blind.'

'Well, yes. There is that. Of course the blindness is

an unwelcome side effect but that hardly ever happens.'

'Much anymore.'

'Yep, much…anymore.'

'Apart from private Skudunkle last week.'

'Good old "Two-patches". Mind you, he's on light-duties now on account of his new perception problem.'

'Lucky bastard.'

'Oy, you.'

The two privates turned to face Eeeek! and the three flyers.

'Oh bugger,' said Albret.

'Right, fat boys,' said Eeeek! 'Up against the wall.'

Albret looked puzzled. 'I'm not fat.'

'That's true,' said Gurted. 'He's just big boned.'

'Shut it, fatty.'

'Hey, what's with all the cacomorphobic talk?' Asked Gurted. 'Just because a guy's a little stout there's no need to get all insulting.'

Plob could see that Eeek! was starting to lose control of the situation so he stepped in. 'Gentlemen, if you could both draw your swords, drop them on the floor in front of you and step back, I am sure that I can persuade the goblin, who doesn't like fat people, to refrain from throwing a knife into your eye.'

'Can we keep our sandwiches?' Asked Albret.

'Yes.'

'Thank you.'

Two rusty, notched swords clanged to the floor and two stout soldiers stepped back a pace.

'Well done,' said Plob. 'Now, we are the enemy and we are here to steal three dragons. If you do as you are told and no harm comes to us then I promise that no harm shall come to you either. Understood?'

Two heads nodded and eight chins wobbled.

'Do you think that you can help us to saddle up three dragons?'

Nod. Wobble.

'Well then, lead on.'

The two Vagoths trundled down the length of the corridor and into the main pens, both still munching on their industrial sized comestibles.

'Here,' said Gurted. 'The dragons on this side have been fed and watered and have already been saddled in preparation for their morning exercise. None have been fired up yet. We only do that after breakfast and the attack has seen that breakfast has been postponed.'

'So what's that you're eating?' Asked Eeeek!

'Preprandial snack, your goblin-ness. Stave off the hunger until the boiled pigs head and dumplings.' Gurted opened up a pen door. 'This one is called *Grossenfuer*, good for you, I think,' he said, pointing at Plob. He moved to the next pen. 'This little girl is named *Winzigerfuer*, good for the pretty lady.' He bowed in Spice's direction. 'This, *Grosshandle*, for you,' he handed the reins to Smudger. 'Now...I suppose that you are going to kill us?'

'Of course not,' said Plob.

'I might,' mumbled Eeeek!

'Well then, kind sirs, may I ask a boon? May you please tie us up so that it does not appear that we have been complicit in this...umm...expropriation of Vagoth military property.'

'I can do better than that,' said Eeeek! 'I can make it look as though you got into a vicious fight trying to stop us.'

'Sounds good,' said Albret. 'How?'

Eeeek! Cocked his arm and punched Albret on the nose. The stout man went down in a welter of snot and blood. Eeeek! Spun around and slammed his elbow into Gurted's temple knocking him to the floor, a black eye already starting to form.

'What?' Said Eeeek! Taking in Plob's disapproving expression. 'I did it for their own good.'

'Yeah, sure.'

'Promise,' continued Eeeek! 'I'm all heart I am. I'm telling you, my good nature will be the death of me someday.'

The three led the dragons out of the pen and into the exercise ring.

'Plob grasped Eeeek! by the hand. 'Many thanks, friend. We'll be off now.'

The three dragon riders mounted up. Eeeek! threw them a quick salute and then stalked away.

Plob thumped his heels into his dragon's flanks and the beast gaited forward and lumbered into the air with the other two close behind. As they gained height Plob could see that the goblins were already retreating back to the safety of the forest. They weren't being harried as the Vagoths were currently more interested in putting out the fires than chasing their foe.

As they approached the extraction point above the forest Plob felt almost anticlimactic. He had achieved what he had set out to do, but now he was spent and it was all that he could do to simply keep himself awake as the adrenalin that had been keeping him going for the last few days simply ran out.

Then he felt the welcomed tug of transference and was gone.

Chapter 31

A gloopy sound. Unpleasant. Biological.

Long frayed strings of mucilaginous mucus oozing from a throbbing amniotic sac suspended by webs from a tree. A being drops from the sac and lies curled on the forest floor. Moonlight reflects off its slime-shiny skin. An ethereal blue glow covers the being in a nimbus of light.

Slowly it rises to its feet. An enlarged head with two big black eyes. Naked, sexless, with smooth grey skin. Child like in stature.

And a voice said, 'I am Nyx; the god of night.

And a second voice said, 'I am Nerus; the god of light.

And yea, a third voice said, 'I am Norgam; the god of all the other bits, including social faux pas, bodily functions, words that rhyme with orange, the infinite universe and fresh milk for the tea.'

And then did the first voice say. 'Hey, hold on. What the hell…we're all in one body!'

'Oh man, that's gross,' said the second voice.

'Sod this for a lark,' said the third voice. 'I'm going to sleep. Wake me up when you guys have made some sort of plan.'

Typhon paraded down the central walkway of the

sacrificial camp cells. All of the cells were packed tight with goblins of various age and sex.

At the front of the cages was a row of stocks with enough space for all of the captives to be lined up, heads secured by the hinged upper block. Then a cunning system of tracks and pulleys could run a heavy blade down the row decapitating all of the goblins in one fell swoop. Detached heads would fall into boxes and sacrificial blood would flow down gutters to the central worshipful-offerings area.

If the prison guards gave it a bit of welly and deigned to work up an actual sweat, then Typhon could see no reason why they shouldn't be able to sacrifice over one thousand goblins an hour. With that rate of immolation the demon lord could hope to transport up to six hundred dragons across the divide in one go. And that would surely tear the bum hole out of Plob and his do-gooder minions.

However, they still needed to collect more goblins before they could go ahead.

'Tell me, Herr Gooballs,' said the big T. 'Those goblins that attacked us this morning. What are you going to do about it?'

'I'm not sure what you mean, Your Bigness.'

'I mean - how are you going to punish them?'

'It's a difficult one, Your Evilness. You see, the loam lord protects the forest. Even flying over it can be dangerous. He has the ability to shoot vast geysers of water to great heights and with deadly accuracy. And if our troops actually venture into the forest they never come back. Ever.'

'Why?'

'Not sure. Some say that the very trees themselves waylay them. Others mention sirens or Dryads. Probably though, they simply get their throats cut by the forest goblins.'

'That won't do. Am I not the Fuhrer of all that I behold?'

'Yes, my leader.'

'And can I behold the forest?'

'Yes again, my leader.'

'Well then, send General Quintus Cerealbox and the ninth legion. They should be able to sort the goblins out, Dryads or no Dryads.'

Gooballs threw one of the new Vagoth salutes, right arm high and palm down. 'I shall tell him at once, my Fuhrer.'

The loam lord stood in the centre of the clearing. He had assumed the humanoid guise that he had established with Plob, judging it to be similar enough to all so as not to create unease. Around him were arrayed the majority of the dominatus level forest goblins. Next to the loam lord stood the holy trinity of goblin gods, three in one.

The forest goblins looked less than impressed.

'So,' said Farticus. 'These are our gods?'

The loam lord nodded.

'Why's there only one of them?'

'There are three,' answered the loam lord. 'But only one body.'

'Why?'

'There is not yet enough belief to sustain three separate bodily entities.'

'And why's it so gloopy? And small?'

'Hey,' said the voice of Nyx. 'Watch your tone. Show some respect or I might smite you.'

'Oh yeah? How?'

The little grey-skinned godly ménage a trios raised its hands and pointed towards Farticus. 'I bring down the wrath of darkness on you and all that you stand for.'

There was a tiny flash of lightening and a burp of thunder. A small rain cloud appeared above Farticus' head, dribbled a little water on him, and disappeared.

'Well,' said Farticus. 'That was scary.'

'Man that was embarrassing,' said the voice of Nerus, god of light. 'I mean, really, could you have been more pathetic if you tried?'

'Hey,' answered Nyx. 'It's not easy, not like the old days. A few hundred years ago that cheeky little gobshite would have been torn to shreds.'

'As opposed to becoming ever so slightly damp?'

'Yeah. As opposed to that.'

A new voice yawned widely. 'Good sleep. Hey, hey, hey, who are all these dudes?'

'They're our worshippers, apparently.' Answered Nerus. 'Nyx has just been busy striking the fear of god into them with an impressive display of damp.'

'Not my fault. We're weak. Not enough faith,' mumbled Nyx.

'Hmm, let me sort this out,' said Norgam.

'It won't work.'

'Trust me. You, the goblin with a smirk on your face. You the leader?'

'We have no leaders,' answered Farticus.

'Yeah, sure, whatever. You guys like fresh milk?'

Farticus looked puzzled. 'Umm…yes.'

'Do you know who I am?'

'Not really.'

'I am Norgam; the god of all the other bits, including social faux pas, bodily functions, words that rhyme with orange, the infinite universe and fresh milk for the tea. And I may be weak but some magiks take little power…so. There you go. All your milk is sour. And until I say otherwise it always will be.'

Farticus flicked a finger at one of the younger goblins that scurried off to the communal kitchens.

He was back in under a minute. He came over to Farticus and whispered in his ear.

'You do not lie, Norgam.'

'Wait. Not finished. Let's try a few social faux pas.' Norgam gestured.

Farticus turned to the goblin next to him. 'Your mother is so ugly, when she tries to take a bath the water jumps out. Oops, sorry. I didn't mean to say that. I know that your mother never baths. What the hell is wrong with me?'

'Do you want me to stop?' Asked Norgam.

'Please!'

'Right, bodily functions. What are your personal views on uncontrollable incontinence?'

'Stop. I believe.' Said Farticus.

'What?'

'I said, I believe.'

'Louder and with feeling.'

'I believe!'

'Louder.'

'I BELIEVE!!'

And he did, for the body housing the transcendental trio grew a foot taller.

'And the rest of you?' Asked Norgam.

'We believe.'

And the body grew again. And then there was a sound liken unto the tearing of the very fabric of the universe.

Then there were three.

Plob was mightily impressed by the amount of work that had been achieved in the last few days.

The artisans, armourers and blacksmiths had all pulled together and had built over two hundred ballistae capable of firing six foot arrows over three thousand feet into the air. These had been grouped around the city in batches of twenty so as to be able to provide a withering quantity of fire at any attacking dragon force.

Biggest had been put in charge of the air defence system.

'When do you tink deys gonna come,' the trogre asked Plob.

'Soon,' replied the young magician.

'How many?'

'It all depends on how many sacrifices Typhon can make. Worse case scenario…five, maybe six hundred dragons.'

'Dat's a lot. Too many, maybe.'

'King Bravad has sent word to all of the four kingdoms. They won't help but at least they'll be ready after we're overwhelmed.'

Biggest gave a chuckle. 'Listen to us. Like a bunch of babies, carrying on like we definitely gonna lose. Maybe we wins…huh? Maybe.'

Plob laughed as well. 'You're right, Big my man, I never thought of that.'

'Though…probably not,' said Biggest.

'Probably not,' agreed Plob.

Chapter 32

General Quintus Cerealbox surveyed his troops. The mighty ninth legion. Four hundred crack troops, battle hardened and fanatically patriotic.

'Ninth legion. Atten…shun!'

Four hundred feet stamped in unison.

'By the left…quick…march.'

Stamp - stamp - stamp. The legion marched from the parade ground, spears held high and sun glittering off their polished shields.

'Ninth legion…regimental song. Sergeant Major, sound off.'

'Yes, sah! Let's hear it boys, loud and proud.'

Our beloved general, he sat on a rock
Shouting and waving his big hairy…
Fist at the ladies who walked on the shore.
Along came a woman who looked like a…
Decent young lady that walked like a duck,
Said she's invented a new way to…
Educate young troopers to sew and to knit.
The soldiers in the barracks were shovelling…
Coal from the cellar and on to the fire
While old adjutant was pulling his…
Horse from the stable and out for a hunt

And his lovely young daughter was powdering her…
Nose and eyelashes while singing this song,
And if you thought it was dirty you're effing well wrong!

'Left, left, left, right, left.'

The Glorious Ninth marched to the edge of the forest with automaton precision…and then stopped.

Because, the problem with the ninth is that they were used to proper warfare. Open plains with thousands of men in squares and phalanxes and lines. With generals surveying the scene from a nearby high vantage point and relaying orders via runners and buglers and dragon riders. And when these criteria were met then the ninth were, without doubt, the dog's bollocks on the battlefield.

But forests really screwed with their brains. One couldn't form a column, nor a square, nor a tortoise. Not even a straight line on account of all the trees getting in the way.

General Cerealbox called a halt and thought for a while. And then, for the first time in the history of the ninth an order was given. Not the usual - 'By the left, quick, advance' no, this order was…

'Ninth,' bellowed general Cerealbox. 'By the left, at your own pace, walk into the forest, watch out for fallen branches and roots and whatnot and try to keep your fellow legionnaires in sight and shout out if you see something.'

There was a slightly confused murmuring amongst the troops and then, in dribs and drabs, they shuffled into the forest. Within a few hundred yards they were no longer the glorious ninth - they were simply four hundred individuals lost in a very thick, dark forest.

Time passed.

Trooper Posterior Rearbutt stopped walking and listened. He hated forests. They were gloomy, and damp, and they had…things that lived in them. And he was sure that he could hear talking, or maybe whispering, right on the edge of his hearing, all the time. He heard a scurrying in the bushes. 'Who's there?'

'Posterior, is that you?'

'Gods, it's Glandular Butoks, have you seen anyone else?'

'No, it's impossible, the woods are too thick. I'm lost.'

'Me too.'

'I'm not.'

'Who said that?' Asked Butoks.

'Me. I said that I'm not lost. Mind you, I haven't actually moved from this spot for over sixty years now, so perhaps I am lost but I'm lost in a place that I know very well. Wow, that's pretty deep that is.'

'Butoks,'

'Yes, Posterior.'

'Have you just developed a talent for ventriloquism?'

'No.'

Well, then I think that this tree is talking to us.'

'Don't be silly, trees don't talk.'

And just like that, Posterior became part of the running gag.

Butoks stared at the evergreen for a while. 'Do you think that it's a spy for the goblins?' He asked Posterior.

'I'm not sure. But we can't take the risk. I think that we should kill it.' Posterior grabbed his battleaxe that was slung over his back and took a swing at the evergreen.

The axe bit deep and the tree cried out in agony. Butoks swung again.

'Oak!' Screamed the evergreen. 'Help me.'

There was a creaking sound, like a thousand squeaky floorboards being stepped on by a thousand assassins deep in the night. And two massive oaken boughs grabbed hold of Butoks and tore him…slowly…in half.

Posterior turned and ran.

'Are you all right?' Rumbled the oak.

'It hurts.'

'You'll heal up, don't worry.'

'Thank you, oak.'

'It's Arthur, remember?'

Thanks, Arthur.'

Halcyon was impressed. So he said so.

'Dude, I'm like, you know, impressed.'

Up close the camouflage sheeting had seemed wrong. Childlike in its rawness. Slashes of brown and grey, thick hanks of rope threaded it through like giant dreadlocks, small pebbles and sand glued to the rest. But when they had taken it down into the valley, and thrown it over a full sized Bulwark and rider, it had rendered them pretty much invisible. Halcyon could see that, without doubt, there was no chance that the dragon riders would be able to see them from the air.

'Right, dudes and dudesses,' said Halcyon. 'I need you to make, like, a thousand of those sheets. Comprehende?'

'Right on, Halcyon. Right on.'

General Cerealbox was in a waking nightmare. The sun had long since gone down and he had not seen any of his men for over three hours.

But he had heard them. Awful sounds. Terrible sounds that started with screams and always seemed to end in several variations of choked off gurgling interspersed with frantic pleas for mercy. But he hadn't even heard any of those for the last hour. In fact, the general suspected that he was the very last of the glorious ninth to still be upright and breathing.

On top of that - the trees were talking. And he was sure that, at some point earlier on, he had seen a bunch of old men with long grey beards and an assortment of weapons, kill three of his troopers whilst sprouting odd passages of philosophical arguments. What more could go wrong?

The ground in front of the general reared up, formed into a humanoid being made out of mud, grasped the general firmly by throat and began to squeeze.

Quintus Cerealbox soiled himself.

Then he died.

Chapter 33

The three gods stood in the clearing. They glowed.
No longer were they a three-in-one deal. And no
longer were they titchy in size, now measuring six
feet each in height. But they were still grey skinned
and large eyed with bulbous triangular shaped heads.
And they were still as sexless as Ken dolls.

The loam lord reared up out of the sod. 'It is over,'
he said.

'We know,' said the gods in unison.

'Are you guys going to always say things together
like that?' Asked the loam lord.

'We speak as one unless we are not together,' said
the three that were once one.

'Well…it's pretty irritating.'

'We know that,' chorused the trinity. 'And now
we need to know, who else is fighting against the
despoilers?'

'The trees have heard, via their twitter network,
that the rockriders of the Rohan have been on the
warpath. Initially they were successful but have now
been pinned down by the Vagoth dragon corps.'

Norgam; the god of all the other bits, including
social faux pas, bodily functions, words that rhyme
with orange, the infinite universe and fresh milk for

the tea, stepped forward. 'I shall travel to see them.'

'How will you get there?' Asked the loam lord.

'I am a god. I shall get there by simply being there.'

He disappeared.

There was a gasp from the surrounding goblins. Truly their gods were all powerful.

Then he appeared again.

'Sorry, forgot to ask for directions. Where actually are the rockriders?'

'Like far out, man,' said Halcyon as he turned to the Honcho. 'Hey, check out the grey dude, Honcho, he like, just appeared, man.'

'Take me to your leader,' ordered Norgam.

'Sure, grey dude, like, here he is.' Halcyon pointed at the Honcho.

'I am Norgam; the goblin god of all the other bits, including social faux pas, bodily functions, words that rhyme with orange, the infinite universe and fresh milk for the tea.'

'You are welcome here, Norgam,' greeted the Honcho. 'However, and I don't want to come over all fascist, man, but these are frantic times, you dig, so, how do we know that you're a god?'

'Yeah,' said Halcyon. 'Like you gotta show us that being a god is your bag, man.'

Norgam looked at the rockriders for a while. And then he spoke. 'What rhymes with orange?'

'Hey,' said Halcyon. 'I, like, know this one, man. Nothing rhymes with orange, it's like, non-copasetic with other words.'

'There is a part of a fern,' said Norgam. 'That is called a sporange.'

Halcyon stared in wonder. 'Orange…Sporange. Hey, grey dude, you are a god.'

'Yes, and we need to talk.'

And so Halcyon told Norgam about how he discovered that the Vagoths were kidnapping entire settlements of goblins and how the rockriders decided to do war upon them as a result. He told of the rockriders' early successes, their following failures and their latest achievements *vis-à-vis* the new camouflage sheets.

Norgam related the tales of the goblin attack whereby Plob and his fellow flyers had stolen some Vagoth dragons and the consequent retributory raid by the once-proud-but-now-defunct-due-to-all-being-dead ninth legion.

'But one thing that we can't figure out, grey god dude,' said Halcyon. 'Is why the Vagoths are taking away all the little green dudes?'

And, in as far as a grey-faced, huge black-eyed, no nostril, tiny-mouthed entity can look sad - Norgam did. 'They are killing my people. Sacrificing them to the dark powers.'

'Whoa, grey god dude,' said Halcyon. 'That's like, super gnarly.'

'Yeah,' agreed the Honcho. 'Bummer to the extreme max.'

'What they, like, sacrificing the little green dudes for, man?'

'They have declared war on Plob's people and in order to cross the divide between here and there they need power. This power can only be gained through the sacrifice of a living being. The more sentient the being the more power gained. In fact, very soon, perhaps only days away, the Vagoth leader is going to perform a mass sacrifice. Perhaps as many as one thousand goblins. By doing this he will garner sufficient power to take over six hundred dragons across the divide. Plob and his people will be annihilated.'

'This is seriously hairy, grey god dude,' said Halcyon. 'I say we split from here and go and give this Vagoth scuzz a beating and save all the little green dudes.'

'Your concern is commendable, rockrider, however, the Vagoth flying corp would destroy you.'

'They wouldn't see us until we were almost there. Our new camo is truly righteous, man.'

'And the moment that they did see you and you were attacked by six hundred dragons?'

Halcyon thought for a moment. 'Well, in that case they would pound us like a group of panty-waisters at a meat fascists BBQ.'

'Exactly - there is no possible way that we can win against Vagoth air superiority.'

'So what do we do, grey god dude?'

'We do the hardest thing that there is…we do nothing. The sacrifices will be made and the Vagoth flyers will be dispatched. And then we shall fall upon the Vagoth army like the wrath of gods. We shall burn their city to the ground, we shall kill every last one of them and then we shall sow their fields with salt and drive away their cattle and poison their wells. When the flyers return there will be nought here for them. They shall be forced to live in a vacuum. No shelter, no food for flyers nor dragons and no water. They will not last a week.'

'Grey god dude, that's like, seriously cold, man. I like it not. It's way harsh.'

'Halcyon, my son,' said the Honcho. 'Remember, those who turn their swords into ploughs will ultimately end up ploughing for those who don't.'

'It is the only way that we can scour this place clean of the Vagoth stain,' said Norgam. 'So what I need you to do is to get your riders as close as possible to the Vagoth city without being detected. Then wait, you will know when the time comes to strike.'

Halcyon nodded his agreement although his heart was heavy with sadness because he knew that, at the end of it all, one could no more win a war than one could win an earthquake.

Chapter 34

London. 13th November 1940.

The Prime Minister rolled the Cuban cigar between his fingers before he put it to his lips and lit up. On his desk in front of him lay a paper flimsy. Across the top, stencilled in bold red in were the words 'Bletchley Park - Top Secret.'

He reread it. Again.

It was short and succinct. 'On the 13th of November approximately five hundred and fifty German bombers are scheduled to hit the town of Coventry. They will strike at nightfall.'

And that was it. Two simple lines that had been decoded by the backroom boys using the newfangled Enigma-decryption techniques.

Winston Leonard Spencer-Churchill knew exactly what he would do. He would contact 12 Group commander Air Vice-Marshal Trafford Leigh-Mallory and Acting Squadron Leader Douglas Bader to get their big wing into the air and see off any attack on the West Midlands city.

He picked up the phone.

He put it down.

If he did that then the Germans would know that the Brits had broken their codes. They would reprogram their blasted Enigma machines and that would be that. No more information. No edge. No advantage. But if he didn't hundreds of innocent people would die. Women. Children.

He picked it up again.

He put it down.

Could he afford to be a humanitarian? Was it not his job, as the leader of a country at war, to be utilitarian?

He picked up the phone again.

He dialled.

'Hello, John. Bring the car around. I'll be travelling to London immediately.'

That evening 515 German bombers hit Coventry. Over 600 people were killed and over two thirds of the historic city was levelled.

In 1945 Winston Churchill went on record to say, the fact that the allies kept secret the breaking of the Enigma code hastened the end of the war by at least two years.

Chapter 35

They say that in war the waiting is the hardest part. This is not true. Dying is the hardest part. Waiting is just...well, waiting.

Biggest sat next to his bundle of arrows and read a letter from home.

Dear Son - this is your mother.
Just a few notes to let you know I am still alive. I am writing this slowly because I know you can't read fast.
You won't know the house when you come home... we moved.
Your sister Bigeena, had a baby this morning. I haven't heard yet
whether it's a boy or a girl, so I don't know whether you're
an aunt or an uncle.
We are all very proud of you and your brothers.
Please try not to die.
Mama xxxx

Master Smegly was grey with exhaustion. He had maintained a magical watch on the inter-dimensional fluxes now for three days and nights without sleep.

And he knew one thing for certain. The sacrifices had started. It was no longer days but hours away.

He watched and he waited.

Science officer Roti and chief engineer Subji had also spent over seventy hours awake, struggling against all odds to find a way of creating enough energy to reverse the polarity of their singularity driven size reversal.

They worked and they waited.

Plob stood in front of his team of dragon riders. His friends. They were the best of the best. He had told them that they were about to face unbeatable odds. He had told them that death was a certainty. And he had told them that they could leave and go home without any stain on their characters. Not one of them had left.

They stood and they waited.

And the sun rose as red as the blood of saints, lightning rent the air and storm clouds did billow and mock the light as darkness came.

The darkness of over six hundred dragon's wings blotting out the sun.

Plob shook hands with each dragon rider before they mounted up. He gave special thanks to the spitfire pilots who, through no fault of their own save their bravery, were going to die again.

'Smudger.'
'Plob.'
'Jonno.'
'Plob.'
'Belter.'
'Plob.'

'Rufin.'

'Do not fear, my friend,' said Rufin. 'We can only do what we can and no more. Always remember; the brave may not live forever - but the cautious never live at all.'

'Rufin - you can talk.'

'Of course I can. Surely you didn't actually think that a man could learn every word in the English language and then not have a clue on how to string at least a few of them together?'

'But why?'

'At the beginning of the war…the last one that I was in, not this one…I lost all of my friends. I vowed never to make friends again and so decided to never speak and thus, never communicate. But, as you can see, it didn't work. Here, around me now, are my dearest friends. Goodbye, Plob, and good luck.'

Rufin walked over to his dragon and mounted up.

Finally, Plob hugged Spice. It was brief. They did not kiss. There was no need; they both knew how they felt.

Plob climbed onto his dragon and clipped on his communication crystal. 'Right, chaps, you know the drill. We climb hard and fast, come at them from out of the sun and don't fire until you see the dandruff on their shoulders. And, in the words of Smudger - relax, no pushing, I'm sure that there's enough of them for everyone.'

The last dragon riders of Maudlin took off and headed towards the enemy.

Chapter 36

Halcyon led the way.

Ten thousand rockriders of Rohan thundered down on the city of the Vagoths. The Honcho had put the colts on the flanks and the larger Bulwarks in the centre. The idea was to encircle the city bar a small escape route on the South side. But waiting behind screens of grass and wood were two thousand goblin slingers and archers who would quickly dispatch anyone who took the obvious escape route.

And standing on a hill overlooking the attack were the three goblin gods.

Halcyon heard the alarms sounding in the city. Bells ringing and bugles blowing. Before the rockriders were within a hundred yards of the walls, a rain of arrows began to fall on them. Thousands of yard long, steel tipped messengers of death. But each rider was equipped with a stout wooden shield that they held above their heads. The thud of arrows slamming into wood carried across the plains like the sound of a great hailstorm. Some of the riders went down but not many.

The Bulwarks struck the wall like a herd of wrecking balls. Cracks appeared in the stone and the Bulwarks pulled back and struck again. And again.

But the walls of the city were thick and strong and had stood for over three hundred years.

Halcyon was on the verge of sounding the retreat when an orgy of lightning rampaged across the walls. Chunks of super-heated stone flew into the air and massive fissures materialised in the walls. Halcyon glanced up at the hill and saw the goblin gods, arms above their heads, surrounded by a pulsating glow of blue-white energy. As he watched them, they collapsed to the ground and the lightning stopped.

'Charge!'

The Bulwarks smashed through the remains of the wall *en masse.* Halcyon crushed a house in his path, his bow ready with arrow notched. But there was no resistance. It seemed as though the defenders on the wall were the only ones.

Halcyon waved his arms ever his head. 'Hold,' he shouted. The riders halted. He beckoned to two of the riders on each side of him. 'Something's, like, not right here. Where's the huge Vagoth army? Like, where are all the defenders, man? You two follow me. The rest of you dudes stay here and stay frosty, okay? Be ready.'

The three Bulwarks trundled down the main street, as they approached the main square the sounds of cheering could be heard, and a brass band. The Bulwarks trundled into the main square to be greeted with the sight of thousands of civilians and military personnel who had discarded their tunics and insignia and weapons. People were singing and shouting.

And, along the one wall of the square, stood three gibbets. Hanging from lengths of hemp were three bodies. A grotesquely obese man in a powder blue tunic, a dwarven hunchback and, what appeared to be a support system for a pair of eyebrows the size of hedgehogs. They were all patently dead.

Two extremely stout men brandishing foot-long sandwiches approached Halcyon.

'Greeting, noble rider of rocks. I am Gurted and this is my companion, Albret. Oh great rejoicing and happiness for you have helped to liberate the city. As you can see, we have already meted out punishment to the leaders most vile.'

'Yes,' said Albret. 'Never again shall man keep his schnapps for many years in a barrel whilst the working classes are forced to drink theirs straight out of the still.'

'Hear, hear,' shouted a man with a patch over each eye and holding a white stick. 'Death to the vintage schnapps drinkers. Down with officers. Blind people rule.'

Gurted held up a sandwich to Halcyon. 'Would you like a sandwich. It's pork knuckle and sour cabbage. Very nice.'

'No, man. I don't eat pork,' answered Halcyon as he tried to work out what schnapps had to do with a mass hanging.

'Why not?'

'I don't know, man. I just don't dig on swine. Listen, where's your leader? Why isn't he doing the hemp fandango?'

Gurted shrugged. 'The Fuehrer has departed. When the lightning struck the walls he conjured a magik and he was gone, like a craven rabbit. Not even bacon?'

'Down with craven, vintage schnapps drinking, rabbits,' shouted the blind man who seemed to have lost his grip on reality along with his eyesight.

'No, not even bacon. So who's in charge?'

'I love bacon,' shouted two-patches. 'It gives me a lardon.'

'I think that Albret and I are. Are you sure you

won't have a pig knuckle sandwich? It's got home made mustard on. Very good.'

'I can see, I can see…oh, wait. No I can't,' said two-patches as he fell over his white cane.

Halcyon shook his head and then looked around. People were throwing flower petals from the higher buildings. A multi-coloured, multi-scented rain of joy scattered across the city.

And Halcyon knew there would be no razing of cities. There would be no poisoning of wells and driving off of cattle and sowing of fields with salt. He had no idea what would happen when the dragon flyers returned but he did know that, at this very moment, there needed to be talk of peace and reconciliation as opposed to talk of hostility and bloodshed.

He climbed down off his Bulwark and shook Gurted by the hand. 'Thank you for your greeting, Gurted. Now, we need to talk.'

Chapter 37

The air was full of fire.

About two hundred Vagoth heavies had peeled off from the main flight and were firebombing the city. Biggest and his entire air defence system had created a cloud of fury, throwing arrow after arrow until there must have been upward of two thousand in the air at the same time. Vagoth dragons screamed and squealed as they fell from the sky, riddled with wood and steel. But there were too many. Balls of burning plasma scoured the city, torching buildings and people alike.

Plob and his riders flew like they had never flown before. They had one small advantage in that, pretty much anything in front of them could be considered the enemy so they fired at will. Vagoth dragons were flying into each other and blasting each other out of the sky as the melee degenerated into a massive orgy of aerial destruction.

Belter was the first Spitfire pilot to go down, hit three times by as many enemies, he pin-wheeled out of the sky and exploded as he hit the ground. Two Maudlin riders followed soon after.

Science officer Roti gabbed engineer Subji by the

shirtfront and smashed him into the wall.

'They are dying out there. Look. Dying - all of them. So do it. It's the only chance that they have.'

'But Roti, if we reverse the polarities by hard wiring the woof engines and reversing the urge power there is every possibility that we shall simply cease to exist.'

'But there is a greater possibility that we will reverse the effects of the black hole and become our normal size again. Do it.'

Captain Bhature walked onto the engine room. 'Gentlemen, what is going on here?'

'Roti wants to blow us all to kingdom-bloody-come,' said Subji.

'Rubbish, all I want is for you to use a short circuit to give us enough power to reverse the singularity.'

'Will this work?' Asked the captain.

'No!' Shouted Subji.

'Yes!' Shouted Roti.

The captain lifted an eyebrow.

'Maybe,' they said together.

'Maybe is good enough for me,' said captain Bhature. 'I'm sick of being titchy. It sucks on a miniscule scale. Wait for me to get to the bridge and then throw the switches.'

Chapter 38

England - September 15th

Over eight hundred German fighters and bombers attacked British air space which was defended by a mere handful of Spitfire and Hurricane fighter pilots.

During the course of that day, which would go on to be known as Battle of Britain day, British pilots claimed over two hundred victories against overwhelming odds. Smudger's ex-squadron was responsible for over two thirds of the kills.

Hitler finally realised that he would never reduce England's air superiority and the invasion of the United Kingdom was called off.

The gratitude of every home in our Island, in our Empire, and indeed throughout the world, except in the abodes of the guilty, goes out to the British airmen who, undaunted by odds, unwearied in their constant challenge and mortal danger, are turning the tide of the World War by their prowess and by their devotion. **Never in the field of human conflict was so much owed by so many to so few.**

Winston Churchill – after the Battle of Britain.

Chapter 39

Plob stood up on his stirrups and dived into the middle of the pack of Vagoths. He had already shot down seven of them and now knew that every fireball might be his last.

Behind him another Maudlin dragon rider went down in a screaming conflagration.

He knew that it was all over. He clicked on his communicator.

'Gentlemen, thank you. We have done all that we can do. May the gods be with you.'

Then there was a sound that defied all description or even meaning. An instant displacement of thousands of cubic feet of air with a combined sucking and blowing and clapping and vibrating.

In short, it was the sound of a twelve-foot long miniature Paratha class starship instantly becoming a full sized four hundred foot long Paratha class starship.

And on the bridge of the starship the captain turned to the science officer. 'Officer Roti, are all weapons in working order?'

'Yes, captain.'

'Can the computers identify friend or foe?'

'Affirmative, captain, they simply use the

communicators as reference.'

'Good, please activate the rotary plasma guns, the electronic arc casters and the wave-particle torpedoes.'

'All weapons are activated and tracking individual targets, captain.'

'On my command, officer Roti...wait...fire all weapons!'

The Vagoth dragon corps ceased to exist.

Chapter 40

And yea, the people of Maudlin did party hard.

For is it not said, forget yesterday, live for today, plan for tomorrow...Party Tonight!

Biggest had taken his magic flask of never-ending blutop and spiced up about a hundred barrels of cider, creating a drink that was so high in alcoholic content it could be used for cleaning the silverware.

At the one end of the city square a troop of musicians was belying out a song that had become very popular amongst the youth of late.

Party like you just don't care
Run around town with your knickers in the air

'I doesn't get dis song,' said Biggest to Plob. 'Surely it should be party like you do care. And what's with da knickers thing?'

Plob laughed. 'I don't know, Big. I think it's just a bit of folderol. Don't worry about it.'

Biggest shrugged and went off in search of some food.

Plob sat down on a bench next to Spice and they watched the revellers for a while. The crew of the Paratha were proving to be very popular amongst the Maudlinians now that they were normal sized. They were polite, charming and happened to be the saviours of all that existed, which probably meant that none of them would be sleeping alone that night.

The surprise of the evening had turned out to be Rufus who had become the most erudite and charismatic of raconteurs and he had a veritable throng of admirers packed around him listening to his tales.

Smudger and Jonno were standing off to one side. Both had been badly affected by the death of their friend Belter and were more than a little subdued.

Plob and Spice stood up and went over to the two Spitfire pilots.

'We owe you a huge debt,' said Plob.

Smudger grinned. 'Not a problem, commander. We do what we do because that's what we do. Nothing asked for and nothing owed, it's been a privilege to get the chance to fight evil once more.'

'I'm truly sorry about Belter.'

'Well, technically, he was already dead, so don't feel bad.'

Suddenly the musicians stopped playing and the general clamour of revelment died to a chorus of whispers.

And through the crowd strode a man, almost seven feet tall, pale of skin and clad in robes of endless night. Behind him walked his son, Stanley.

He stopped in front of Plob. 'I have come to collect,' he said.

Rufin walked over to join Smudger and Jonno, and together the three of them stepped forward.

'A deal's a deal,' said Smudger. 'Let's go.'

Plob stepped between Death and the pilots. 'No!'

Silence. Even the wind had stopped.

Death raised an eyebrow. 'No? You dare to defy me?'

'I do. It's not fair.'

Death nodded his head in agreement. 'You are correct, it is not fair, however, it is what will be done.'

'These men have already died once, to take them again would be worse than cruel...it's inhumane.'

'I am not human...I am Death. A covenant was struck and now the time has come for recompense. Stand aside.'

Plob drew his sword. 'No.'

Death laughed. It was the most terrifying sound that Plob had ever heard.

The master of mortality snapped his fingers and Plob fell to the ground, his body wracked with pain. 'Boy,' growled Death. 'You disappoint me.'

And slowly. Ever so slowly. Plob stood up, his face set in a rictus of agony. He lifted his sword again. The tip wavered erratically. 'They stay,' he grunted through clenched teeth.

Stanley stepped forward. 'Father, stop. He has the right of challenge. That is the rule. Plob, put the sword down, you're being ridiculous.'

'I'm asserting my right to challenge.'

'No you're not,' said Stanley. 'You're just being stupid. You can't fight Death on account of...well...him being Death. He will always win. But you can challenge him to a game. The winner gets to keep the souls.'

'Do I get to choose the game?'

'Yes.'

'But not chess,' said Death. 'It's just so clichéd. I really don't think that I could stand another game of chess.'

'Fine,' said Plob. 'Poker. Five-card draw. I win, the boys stay, you win, they go.'

Death grinned. 'Done.'

Boy came forward with a pack of cards. Biggest

pulled up a table and two chairs. The two protagonists sat. Stanley dealt.

Smudger lit his pipe. 'Well, I must say, this is the first time that I've been a pot in a game of poker. I feel a little bit tawdry to be honest.'

'I had a dog once that could play poker,' said Rufin.

'Really,' answered Smudger. 'Was he any good?'

'No, every time he got a good hand he would wag his tail.'

'Bit of an obvious tell, I hope that Plob's better than that.'

'Probably…after all, at least he doesn't have a tail.'

Stanley dealt the cards and the players held them close to their chests.

Plob fanned them out and took a look. Two Kings, a three, a seven and a nine. He threw three cards into the middle.

'Plob takes three cards,' said Stanley as he dealt them out.

Death cast two cards in.

'The Man who rides the pale horse, both Alpha and Omega, Anubis, Yama and Thanatos, Reaper of souls and separator…'

'Stanley!'

'Dad?'

'Shut it.'

'Sorry…Death takes two cards.'

'Right,' said Death. 'Let's see what you have, boy.'

'No.'

'What?'

'I raise you.'

'You cannot raise me. You have nothing that I would want.'

'I raise you…my soul.'

There was a ripple of Ooh's through the crowd and one of the musicians plucked a single drawn out note on his slide guitar. Peeyo-wow-wowwww.

'In return for what?'

'Belter's life. He died in the last battle.'

Death thought for a while. 'You go too far, child. I am not a god, I neither give nor take life.'

'But you can.'

'Already I have bent the rules to breaking point.'

'He sacrificed his all for a people that he did not know. He is a hero.'

'True, but show me a hero and I will show you a tragedy. My boy, in the infinities of time I have seen many heroes, good men who have given all that they can give so that others may live better lives. Thankfully, true heroes are more common than one thinks. Should I give all of these people life again?'

Plob closed his eyes for a while. 'My soul…Belter's life.'

Death stared, silently.

'Please,' said Plob.

And an infinity of devotion and duty and sorrow looked at the young magician. And decided.

'It shall be done. Now show your stuff, child.'

With shaking hand Plob laid them out. A seven…and four kings.

Death raised an eyebrow.

And then he stood and looked around him. He looked at the crowd and saw every single person there. He looked into their pasts and their futures and their children's, childrens futures. And he saw joy and pain and suffering without end. And love. Above all, he saw love.

'You have won.' He said. Then he snapped his fingers and Belter appeared, lying on the floor next to them. 'He is merely sleeping, allow him to wake naturally.' Death laid his cards face down on the table and stood up. He held out his hand to Plob. 'Well done, commander, you are a brave man. Foolhardy but brave. I can see why my son likes you so much. Come, Stanley, we leave.'

The light dimmed. Death and son were gone.

The crowd went wild.

And yea, the people of Maudlin did party even harder than before. The pilots held Plob high on their shoulders and paraded him around the square to the tumultuous applause of the people of Maudlin. Men rushed forward to shake his hand and women threw kisses. And sometimes, other things of a more frilly and feminine nature.

Much later, the sun rose at the same time that the revellers decided to call it a night.

Biggest stood alone, watching the massive ball of fire crawl over the horizon as it began its daily march across the heavens. He sat down at a nearby table, lit up a cigar the size of a baby's arm and took a deep drag. On the table on front of him lay Death's losing hand of cards, face down. Biggest idly turned them over.

Four aces.

He smiled.

Epilogue

Typhon had no idea where he was. When the rockriders of the Rohan had breached his defences he had summoned what magic he had left over from the mass sacrifices and simply leapt to…somewhere else.

It was a city of some sort. Some sort of horseless vehicle clattered past. Typhon had seen similar ones outside Hitler's bunker when he had occasioned there once before. The car stopped and the driver got out, ran around to the other side of the car and opened the door. A man in a hat and well fitted suit stepped onto the pavement.

It was then that Typhon noticed that there were three men lurking in the shadows nearby him. They were all carrying similar bang-sticks to what the nazi soldiers had carried. They saw him at the same time that he saw them. They scurried over to him.

'Hey, you are one ugly goon. Tell you what, skedadle out of here before I throw some lead your way, capish?'

Typhon dragged the weapon out of the man's hands and smashed him on the head with it. Without pause he carried on the movement, taking out both of the other thugs in under two seconds. When he looked up, the man in the suit was staring at him.

Both he and the driver had bang-sticks in their hands.

'Pally,' said the man in the suit. 'Looks like you just saved my life. So, what's your story, morning glory, are you wearing a mask or what?'

'No,' rumbled the big T.

'Well, no never mind to me. I owe you'se one, big guy. And let it never be said that Alphonse Gabriel Capone don't pay his debts. Here, you come with me. Let's talk.'

So Typhon, the mother of all-evil, climbed into the car with Al Capone.

And the universe shuddered.

4846158R00113

Printed in Great Britain
by Amazon.co.uk, Ltd.,
Marston Gate.